THE PET FINDERS CLUB

THE PET FINDERS CLUB

THE PET FINDERS CLUB

Searching for Sunshine

BEN M. BAGLIO

Hodder Children's Books

A division of Hachette Children's Books

Special thanks to Liss Norton

Text copyright © 2005 Working Partners Ltd
Illustration copyright © 2008 Cecilia Johansson

First published in the USA in 2005 by Scholastic Inc

First published in Great Britain in 2008
by Hodder Children's Books

The rights of Ben M Baglio and Cecilia Johansson to be identified
as the Author and Illustrator of the Work respectively have been
asserted by them in accordance with the Copyright, Designs and
Patents Act 1988

1

ISBN 978 0 340 93135 6

Typeset in Weiss by Avon DataSet Ltd,
Bidford on Avon, Warwickshire

Printed in the UK by CPI Bookmarque, Croydon, CR0 4TD

The paper and board used in this paperback by Hodder Children's
Books are natural recyclable products made from wood grown in
sustainable forests. The manufacturing processes conform to the
environmental regulations of the country of origin.

Hodder Children's Books
a division of Hachette Children's Books
338 Euston Road, London NW1 3BH
An Hachette Livre UK company

Chapter One

The parcel was waiting for Andi Talbot when she came home from school. "It's from Dad!" she whooped, recognizing his writing on the large brown envelope.

Buddy, Andi's Jack Russell terrier, came bounding out of the living room at the sound of her voice.

Andi bent down to pat him. "Hello, Bud. Have you been good?"

"Good as gold, apart from getting under my feet all day," Andi's mum joked, appearing in the kitchen doorway. "Sometimes I wonder why I take days off. Looking after Buddy is far more tiring than office work."

Andi laughed. She knew her mum loved Buddy almost as much as she did.

1

"What's your dad sent you?" Mrs Talbot asked.

Andi tore open the package. It contained a letter, a packet of seeds, and a large white envelope. She scanned the letter quickly. "Dad's sent my birthday present early because he's going to be away on my birthday." She sighed. "I'd hoped he'd come to England for my birthday. I haven't seen him for ages. I wish he didn't have to work so hard." Her dad lived in Texas, where Andi, her mum and Buddy had been living until several months ago.

Mrs Talbot gave Andi a hug. "He'll come and see you as soon as he's got some holiday, I'm sure. What else does he say?"

Andi turned to the letter again. "These are for you." She handed the seeds to her mum. "Lemon balm. Dad says you should grow them by the back door so you'll brush against them every time you go outside. He thinks you'll like the lemony smell." Andi's parents had been divorced for three years now, but she loved the fact that they still got on well.

"That's kind of him," Mrs Talbot said. "What's in the envelope?"

Andi tore it open. "Oh! Fantastic!" It contained a

brochure for the Riverside Stables. They were located just outside Aldcliffe, the suburb of Lancaster where Andi and her mum lived, and there was a book of twelve vouchers for Western riding lessons with the brochure. Andi's dad had taken her trail riding in the Rocky Mountains during the summer holidays, just before she'd moved to England for her mum's new job. Even though she'd known it was the last time she'd see her dad for quite a while, Andi had had a wonderful time. "I can learn to ride properly now!" she announced with a grin. "And if I learn Western riding, I'll look like a real cowgirl."

The oven timer beeped and Mrs Talbot hurried into the kitchen.

Andi picked up Buddy's favourite squeaky rubber bone and tossed it along the hall. "Fetch, Bud."

Buddy bounded after it. He snatched it up, came racing back to Andi and dropped it at her feet.

"Good boy." Andi ruffled his ears, then threw the bone again. As Buddy charged away, she sat down on the stairs and flipped through the brochure. There were loads of photos of cute ponies being ridden along bridle paths, and there was a picture of a big outdoor arena, too. "These stables look amazing!" she called to her mum. "Can I start this Saturday morning?"

Her mum came out of the kitchen. "Well, I don't know, Andi."

"What's wrong with me going riding on Saturday mornings?"

"You always take Buddy for a long run then. You know how it works. I come home from work at lunchtimes during the week to give him a quick walk, but he's your responsibility at weekends."

"I'll only be riding for an hour or so." Andi couldn't understand why her mum was making so much of it. She was sure Buddy wouldn't mind having his walk later in the day.

"But getting there and back is going to take time," Mrs Talbot said. "You know I go to the supermarket on Saturday mornings."

"We can go shopping any time!" Andi hated arguing, but her mum knew she'd wanted to learn to ride properly ever since her trail riding holiday.

Mrs Talbot sighed. "Perhaps we can sort something out. How about if you take Buddy for a shorter walk on Saturday afternoons, after you've ridden, and a really long one on Sundays?"

"Whatever!" Andi said, still annoyed. "I can find a bus that goes near the stables if shopping's so important. And I'll take Buddy with me." She stomped upstairs with the little Jack Russell trotting behind her.

"Andi, I don't like you speaking to me like this! You're not behaving like someone who deserves riding lessons!" her mum called after her.

Andi didn't reply. She went into her mum's study and slammed the door. She'd been so thrilled at the thought of learning to ride, but her mum's reaction had been like a cold shower. "You won't mind if I go riding, will you, Bud?" she asked, sitting down at the computer.

Buddy flopped down across her feet with a contented sigh.

Andi stroked his ears, then switched on the computer. "I'll email Dad, to thank him for the present." She paused, thinking about the row between her and her mum. "And then I'd better go downstairs and apologize."

* * *

5

"Guess what!" Andi yelled, racing across the playground to join her best friends, Natalie and Tristan, next morning.

"Another case?" Natalie asked excitedly.

"Excellent!" Tristan said. He flung down his rucksack with a groan. "This thing weighs a ton. Miss Ashworthy's gone homework mad!"

"It's good for you, Tris," Natalie said. "You don't want your brain seizing up." She turned to Andi, her blue eyes shining. "So tell us all about it. Are the Pet Finders in business again?"

Andi, Natalie and Tristan ran the Pet Finders Club to track down lost animals. They'd met up when Andi had lost Buddy just after moving to Aldcliffe from Texas. They made a great team — especially as Tristan had a photographic memory and Natalie had some great contacts — and had already tracked down a whole load of missing pets.

"It's not a new case," Andi said. "My dad's bought me some riding lessons."

Natalie wrinkled her nose. *"Riding lessons?"*

"Western riding, like cowboys do. I loved trail riding in the Rocky Mountains," Andi explained. "My dad took me last summer."

Natalie tossed back her blonde hair. "Trail riding's OK, I guess. I had a go when I was on holiday in America. I didn't know you could learn how to do it round here."

"Riding's way too dangerous," Tristan said. "People fall off horses and break their arms and stuff."

Andi raised her eyebrows at him. "Not like skateboarding then," she said with mock seriousness. "Nobody *ever* gets hurt falling off a skateboard." Tristan spent half his life glued to a skateboard and the other half coming unglued in a fairly spectacular way. Just now, he had a plaster on his chin and one on each hand to show for his most recent falls. Andi was pretty sure he'd have cut knees and elbows, too, but they were hidden by his jacket and jeans.

"It's hardly the same thing," Tristan began. Before he could say anything else, the bell rang for the start of school.

Natalie linked arms with Andi. "Come on, Annie Oakley. Hitch your horse and let's get into school."

"I can hardly wait to get on a pony again!" Andi exclaimed for the millionth time on Saturday morning, as she, her mum and Buddy headed for the riding stables. Her mum had agreed to let her go riding on Saturdays after Andi apologized for being rude and promised to make sure Buddy got enough attention in the afternoon.

Buddy was standing on Andi's lap, gazing out of the window. He seemed to sense Andi's excitement because every few seconds he gave a little high-pitched bark.

Andi hugged him. "Is it much further, Mum?"

"I think we're almost there." Mrs Talbot met her eyes in the rear-view mirror. "Poor Buddy, he thinks he's going for a walk."

"I'll take you for a walk this afternoon, Bud," Andi told him, rubbing his tummy.

Buddy licked her nose.

They were right out in the countryside now, with fields on either side. The trees were almost bare; only a handful of yellow leaves still clung to the branches. The mountains loomed up ahead, their craggy tops hidden by low clouds. Andi's excitement grew. The Lake District mountains were one of the things she liked best about living in Lancaster – they were so different to anything she'd seen in Texas.

She pointed ahead suddenly. "Look!" A wooden sign standing by the roadside read: RIVERSIDE STABLES. It was decorated with pictures of horses, and a black arrow showed that they had to turn right.

Mrs Talbot turned on to a stony track that sloped steeply uphill. Ahead, Andi could see a collection of old red-roofed buildings. Beyond the buildings, sloping grassy fields stretched away to the pine forest. In one, a herd of red-and-white cows were grazing; in another, a huddle of ponies stood close together. Further off still, the mountains rose up and up until they met the sky.

They drove into the yard and parked near an L-shaped stable block. Andi watched eagerly as two girls a little older than her came out of a stable, leading a brown pony. *That'll be me soon*, she thought with a thrill of excitement. Another girl appeared carrying a saddle. "Hang on, you two," she called, hurrying after her friends.

On the far side of the yard were a bungalow and a large barn. A woman about Mrs Talbot's age, wearing a battered windcheater and with tousled black hair, came out of one of the stables. "Hello there," she called. "Welcome to Riverside Stables. I'm Mrs O'Connor, the owner."

"Hello. I've got a voucher for a riding lesson."

Mrs O'Connor smiled. "You must be Andi Talbot."

"That's right." Buddy jumped out of the car, his tail wagging enthusiastically.

"He's a cute little ball of energy!" Mrs O'Connor bent down to stroke Buddy's ears. "But keep him on his lead, won't you? We've got livestock here."

"OK." Tightening her grip on Buddy's lead, Andi looked round. She counted fifteen stable doors. Most of them were closed, but a dappled grey horse was looking out of the nearest stable. Andi went over to stroke him. "Aren't you a beauty?" she murmured, rubbing his nose.

The horse nuzzled her hand as though he hoped she might have a titbit.

"Let's go and put Andi's lessons on the calendar, Mrs Talbot," said Mrs O'Connor.

"I won't be long, Andi," Mrs Talbot called.

Andi smiled over her shoulder. "Bud and I will go and explore." She said goodbye to the horse, then headed for the barn. Inside, to her astonishment, was a herd of small black-and-white goats. "These don't look much like horses," she laughed.

Buddy scampered up to the goats' pen, pulling Andi behind him. "They're goats, Bud," she told him. "You've probably never seen one before."

A young goat was leaning against the fence. It jumped away when Buddy appeared, then tiptoed back to stare curiously at him through the rails.

"It's OK." Andi reached over the fence to stroke the goat. "He won't hurt you." To her surprise, the goat's fur was soft and silky; she'd expected it to feel much coarser.

The goat reared up on its hind legs and rested its front hooves on the fence. "Aren't you pretty?" Andi said. The goat turned its head and tried to nibble her sleeve. Laughing, Andi drew her hand back. The goat bleated.

The sound must have startled Buddy because he began to bark. The goat skittered away from the fence.

"Be quiet, Buddy!" Andi scolded. She scooped him up and carried him out of the barn.

A dark-haired girl of about eighteen was leading two ponies across the yard. One was a small shaggy

12

brown mare; the other was a sturdy chestnut with three white socks. A blonde, round-faced boy aged about ten and a girl a couple of years younger, who looked so like him that she had to be his sister, were watching them eagerly.

"I hope the little one's mine!" the girl exclaimed. "She's so cute!"

Andi crossed the yard, wondering where her mum had got to. Suddenly she spotted a white duck with a yellow bill waddling along a passage that ran between the barn and the end of the stable.

Buddy spotted the duck, too. He wriggled furiously in Andi's arms.

"Hold still, boy!" Andi gasped.

Buddy squirmed even more. Andi couldn't keep hold of him a moment longer. He dropped to the ground and charged away, barking loudly. Andi stamped on the end of his lead, but it slid out from under her foot.

"Buddy!" she yelled, racing after him. "Come back!"

Buddy disappeared round the corner and Andi heard an explosion of quacks. She burst out of the passage in time to see him leaping into a duck pond.

Muddy water flew up round him and the ducks scattered in all directions.

Andi was horrified. "Buddy! Come here!"

He ignored her and stayed in the pond, barking madly as though he was having the best game ever.

"Buddy!" Andi yelled again.

Suddenly a dark-haired boy came pelting round the side of the barn. "What on earth do you think you're doing?" he demanded, splashing into the pond. He caught Buddy by the collar and hauled him out. "Imagine letting a dog loose! Are you out of your mind?"

"I'm sorry," Andi began. "He—"

The boy didn't let her finish. "You shouldn't be in charge of a dog. You obviously don't know a thing about animals!"

Andi was furious. "For your information, I know lots about animals!"

"Oh yeah? Well, it doesn't look like it from where I'm standing." The boy thrust Buddy's lead into Andi's hand and stalked away.

Chapter Two

Andi glared after the boy. She was about to charge after him and tell him exactly what she thought of him, when Buddy jumped up and planted his muddy paws on her jeans. "Oh, Buddy!" she scolded.

She pushed him down and held him on a short lead. Then, crouching beside him, she pulled up a handful of long grass and began to rub at the mud that coated his legs and tummy.

Buddy licked her nose.

"You're not getting away with that this easily. I can't believe you showed me up like that, chasing those poor ducks!"

The handful of grass was soon caked in mud and Buddy looked no cleaner than before. Andi threw it down. "Let's get you back to the car." She hoped she wouldn't see the boy again as she led Buddy along the passage. To her relief there was no sign of him in the yard.

Keeping a tight grip on Buddy's lead, she crossed the yard quickly, trying not to look at any of the other riders. Buddy was so filthy they'd probably all be staring. Reaching the car, she opened the boot and took out the old towel she kept there. Buddy seemed to have a homing instinct for muddy puddles and Andi regularly had to rub him down when they'd been for a long walk.

She was halfway through drying him when her mum came out of Mrs O'Connor's office. "All done," she said. "And your lesson's . . ." She trailed off. "Oh, Andi. What's Buddy been up to now?"

Andi told her about the duck pond without mentioning the dark-haired boy. She felt a bit guilty, because she should have known better than to let Buddy chase the ducks.

Mrs Talbot sighed. "I knew something like this would happen. Buddy's used to running off his energy with a long walk on Saturday mornings."

Andi didn't want to hear this all over again. She heard a horse's hooves behind her and she glanced round. The dark-haired girl was walking towards her leading a buckskin pony. "Hello there. Are you Andi?"

"That's right."

The girl smiled. "I'm Shona, your group leader. We're ready for you now. This is Sunshine, the pony you'll be riding."

Andi looked at the copper-coloured mare. She had a pale-grey mane and tail and huge, friendly brown eyes. "She's definitely the best sunshine I've seen in Lancaster so far," she joked.

Shona laughed. "Do you want to come and tack her up?"

"You bet!" Andi had loved fitting Clancy's saddle and bridle when she'd been trail riding in the Rockies. It had made her feel like a *real* rider.

As Shona led the pony forward, Andi noticed that there was a dark streak in her tail. "That's unusual, isn't it?" she said.

"Well, I've never seen another buckskin with a tail like it. But it's pretty, don't you think?"

"Oh, yes." Andi quickly wiped the last trace of

mud from Buddy's coat. She opened the car door and he jumped in. "See you later, Bud," she said, leaning in to stroke him. He looked unhappily up at her and began to whine. "It's OK, boy. I'll only be gone an hour."

She shut the car door and Buddy flopped down on the seat with his head on his paws. Andi felt a stab of guilt and turned away quickly. *Buddy will enjoy going to the garden centre with Mum,* she told herself. He loved trotting along the aisles and sniffing all the plants.

"Enjoy your ride," Mrs Talbot said.

"I will! See you in an hour." Andi took the pony's reins, suddenly feeling a bit nervous.

"Sunshine will look after you," Shona said, as if she'd noticed Andi's expression change. "She's really good-natured. You've already done some riding, is that right?"

"Yes. I went trail riding in the Rocky Mountains with my dad before I came to live in England."

Shona's smile broadened. "Lucky you! I'd love to do that." Then she frowned. "Did you live in America then? I'd never have guessed. You sound English to me."

Andi shrugged. "My mum's English. I must have her accent."

"Well, I'm still dead jealous," Shona said, laughing. "Trail riding in the Rocky Mountains is my idea of heaven. Now, come and meet your group." She strode across the yard towards the blonde boy and girl. Four ponies and a horse were tied to a rail, and the girl was hugging the shaggy pony as though she didn't ever want to let go. Another boy, thin and wiry and aged about eleven, was tightening the girth on a sorrel pony. The pony's light-chestnut coat was flecked with white that looked a bit like snowflakes.

Andi kept pace with Shona, and Sunshine walked willingly beside her.

"We're going on a trail ride today so I can assess you before we ride in the school," Shona explained. "Trail riding is a really good way to meet the horses, and there's all this beautiful scenery, too."

Andi gazed up at the mountains. "You can say that again!"

"Meet Andi, everyone," Shona said as they joined the rest of the group. "This is Tim and Helen." She waved a hand towards the blonde kids. "Helen's riding Scrumpy and Tim's on Bonnie. And this is Darryl and Chipper." She patted the sorrel pony. "How are you doing with that girth?" She checked the strap that held Chipper's saddle in place. "Great! You've done a good job."

Darryl smiled. "Thanks."

"Now, you need to fetch Sunshine's saddle, Andi. Tie her to the rail first."

Andi looped the reins round the rail and tied them securely. She didn't want her pony running off. Trying to catch Buddy had been bad enough!

"There's the tack room." Shona pointed. "The saddle's on your right as you go inside. You'll see Sunshine's name on the shelf."

Andi found the saddle easily and lifted it down. By the time she got back to the group, another girl had joined them. She was very tall, a good head taller than Andi – though she didn't look much older – and her fair hair was cropped short. She was wearing a pair of jodhpurs, close-fitting riding trousers that were so well worn that the seat and the inside of the thighs were shiny. She was stroking Sunshine.

"Hello," Andi said. "I'm Andi."

"I'm Sara." The girl glanced briefly at Andi, then turned back to Sunshine.

Andi placed the saddle on Sunshine's back.

"What are you doing?" Sara asked sharply. "I want to ride this pony."

Andi looked at her in surprise. "But Shona said—"

Sara didn't let her finish. "I mean, she's so cute," she added, sounding a bit more friendly.

"Actually, Sara, you're on Tilly," Shona said. "You're a more experienced rider than Andi, and Tilly isn't suitable for a novice."

Tilly was tied to the other end of the rail. She was the best-looking of all the ponies: reddish-brown with a black mane and tail. Sunshine was adorable, but Tilly was even more striking. Andi was sure Sara would be pleased to ride her.

Sara hardly glanced at Tilly. "Please let me ride Sunshine," she begged.

Shona looked surprised. "I'm sorry, but Sunshine really is much more suitable for Andi. Maybe you can ride her another time." She lifted Sunshine's saddle flap and examined the buckles that held the girth in place. "Well done, Andi," she said. "Have a look, everyone. Andi's done a great job with this girth."

The other riders crowded round.

"She's cinched it tight," Shona went on, "but with just enough room to slip her hand underneath and smooth down Sunshine's hair behind her front leg. Any tighter and Sunshine wouldn't be able to breathe or move comfortably. Any looser and the saddle would slip." She looked up and smiled at everyone. "OK. Let's mount up! Does anyone need a hand? Helen?"

"I can manage, thanks," Helen replied. She placed one foot in a stirrup and hauled herself up. Shona guided her other foot into the second stirrup and the little girl sat up straight, grinning with delight.

Andi unhitched Sunshine from the rail and swung herself into the saddle. It felt good to be on a horse again, and she tried to remember all the things she'd learnt during her holiday. She sat deep in the Western-style saddle, letting her legs hang comfortably, and held the reins lightly in her right hand.

Sara finished saddling Tilly and mounted

without looking at Andi or Sunshine.

Shona climbed on to her long-legged horse. Her reddish-brown coat was spotted with grey, and she had a black mane and tail. "Your horse is pretty, Shona," Andi said. "What do you call that colour?"

"Harley is a roan. It's my favourite colour." Shona patted Harley's neck. "Now, let's go!" She led the way round the side of the stables. Andi waved to her mum and Buddy, then followed.

They skirted the edge of the field with the red-and-white cows, keeping to a path that ran next to a river. The paddock where the ponies grazed sloped uphill and the gate at the far end led right into the forest that covered the mountainside. Andi felt a tingle of excitement as they rode towards the pine trees, the ponies' hooves thudding softly on the grass.

Shona rode in front with Helen. The little girl was chattering about how much she loved ponies and how she wanted to have her own one day. Darryl and Tim rode side by side, not talking much. Behind them rode Sara. Andi stopped to shut the paddock gate and fell a little way behind. She gave

Sunshine a gentle kick and the pony began to trot. Andi leant forward to pat her neck as she stood up and sat down in time to Sunshine's stride. She was glad she hadn't forgotten how to post to the trot: her holiday seemed ages ago.

As she came alongside Sara, the girl looked round. "It's great out here, isn't it?" Andi said eagerly, reining Sunshine to a walk.

"Yeah, I suppose so."

"Have you done a lot of riding?" Andi persisted, trying to get a conversation going.

"Yeah, quite a lot." Sara didn't look up at her; instead, she was staring at Sunshine's flank.

"Er, is there something wrong with my stirrups?" Andi asked.

Sara looked surprised. "No, why?"

"I thought you were looking at them just now. Maybe I'm not sitting right, is that it?" Andi sat straighter in the saddle.

"No, you're fine," Sara said. They rode on in silence for a while.

Andi noticed that Sara kept shooting sideways glances at her. "Am I holding the reins right? Todd, the group leader when I went trail riding in the

25

Rockies, said ponies should have a bit of slack in Western riding. Am I giving Sunshine enough? Or too much?"

Sara shrugged. "About right, I'd say."

"Have you been to Riverside Stables before?"

"No."

Andi began to feel uncomfortable. She wondered if Sara was jealous of her because she was riding Sunshine. But Shona had already said she could ask to ride Sunshine next time.

They reached the edge of the wood and Shona halted. She turned round in her saddle. "Well done, everyone. Great riding so far! Tim, don't forget to keep your reins loose – you don't need to keep a contact on the bit all the time."

They entered the wood in single file because the path was so narrow. Andi rode at the back. The path was thick with fallen pine needles, and the ponies' hooves made almost no sound. A few birds sang and once a squirrel chattered at them as they passed.

Rounding a bend in the path, they came upon a fallen tree, its trunk green with moss. Tilly shied away from it, snorting. Sara sat very still and closed her legs against the pony's flanks. After a couple of steps, Tilly calmed down.

"Wow, you're a really good rider!" Andi said admiringly.

Sara didn't reply. She glanced at Sunshine, then rode on again. Andi followed, more puzzled than ever.

They came out of the wood on to a stretch of grass dotted with spindly trees. On the far side lay a massive boulder. Andi wondered if it had broken away from the mountain years ago and bounced and rolled its way down before coming to a stop here.

Ahead of them, a river glittered in the autumn sunshine. "This river gave Riverside Stables its name," Shona explained. "It vanishes underground in a cave higher up the mountain, near those old buildings." She pointed out a cluster of ramshackle barns that clung to the slope about quarter of a mile above them. The buildings were precariously perched on the very edge of a steep cliff. Even from this distance Andi could see that they were ruins, with holes in the roofs and walls.

"What are they?" Darryl asked.

"That's Riverside Farm. It was built by Polish immigrants about thirty years ago, but the floods have eroded the ground and the buildings are too dangerous to use now. If any more ground falls away, they'll go with it. The road to the farm is dangerous, too, especially in bad weather. It's really steep and rocky." Shona shivered. "I always think the place looks haunted."

Andi stayed where she was for a few moments, looking up at the old farm. Living in such an isolated place would have been pretty scary, even if the buildings hadn't been hanging on the edge of a cliff. Shona was right: it *did* look haunted, like an old film set. Andi could just imagine the ghost of the farmer stumbling round on a stormy winter's night, searching desperately for the possessions he had lost in the flood . . .

She grinned, realizing that sounded like the sort of thing Tristan might say, then urged Sunshine into a trot to catch up with the others.

She soon reached the enormous rock. As she trotted past, a brownish snake with a black zigzag pattern on its back slithered down from it. Sunshine leapt back with a shrill whinny of fright.

"Whoa, girl!" Andi gasped. She tried to shorten the reins, but Sunshine jerked her head and snatched them out of Andi's hands.

A moment later, she was bolting across the grass at top speed!

Chapter Three

Terrified, Andi scrambled for the reins and pulled hard. But Sunshine was thoroughly spooked and didn't break her stride as she galloped uphill. Andi felt herself slipping sideways in the saddle and buried her hands in Sunshine's mane. She flashed past Shona and the other riders, catching a glimpse of their shocked faces.

"Hang on, Andi! I'm coming!" Shona yelled.

Sunshine streaked full tilt towards the river. Still clinging on for dear life, Andi prayed the pony would stop once she reached the water. But to her dismay Sunshine charged through the shallows, her hooves crunching over the pebbles. She leapt out on the other side and galloped on.

Andi shut her eyes, feeling dizzy with fear.

Suddenly she heard different hoof beats. Cautiously she opened her eyes. A pale horse was almost level with her. The rider leant out of the saddle and caught Sunshine's reins. "Easy, girl."

Sunshine slowed down as the reins went taut: first to a canter, then to a trot and finally to a walk.

Shakily, Andi straightened up and turned to her rescuer, wanting to thank him. She opened her mouth, but nothing came out. It was the boy from the stables who had shouted at her about Buddy chasing the ducks.

"What on earth were you doing? You need to keep control of your pony," he snapped, glowering down at her.

"It wasn't my fault!" Andi retorted indignantly. "A snake frightened her."

"Of course it was your fault!"

Shona cantered up, her face pale. "Andi, are you all right?"

"Yes, thanks. Just a bit shaky."

"Thank goodness you managed to hold on. And thank goodness you were nearby, Neil. I don't know what might have happened if you hadn't stopped Sunshine when you did."

Andi patted Sunshine's slippery neck. She didn't trust herself to say anything more; she certainly wasn't about to act as though Neil was any kind of hero. The pony was calmer now; she'd stopped trembling and was reaching up to touch noses with the boy's horse. Andi noticed that it was a palomino, a pale-tan horse with a silver mane and tail.

"Andi, this is Neil O'Connor," Shona added. "He's Mrs O'Connor's son. And Neil, this is Andi Talbot."

Neil tightened his grip on Sunshine's reins. "I suppose we'd better get her back to the group. You go on ahead, Shona. I'll look after Andi."

"I don't need looking after, thank you very much," Andi snapped, when Shona had gone.

Neil grinned unexpectedly, his teeth white against his tanned skin. "That's not how it looks to me. Now hold on to Sunshine's mane, so you don't fall off." He set off along the trail at a trot, leading Sunshine by her reins.

As the pony started forward, Andi felt herself slipping. Hurriedly, she twisted her fingers into Sunshine's mane again. It would be totally humiliating to fall off now. "You don't need to lead me along," she hissed. "I'm not a complete novice, you know."

Neil ignored her.

"Give me back my reins!" Andi said angrily.

He didn't even glance back, and Andi had no choice but to jog along behind him, feeling angry and shaken and generally fed up. She was beginning to wish her dad hadn't bought her riding lessons after all!

Mrs Talbot was waiting by the car when Andi and the other riders came clattering into the yard. Buddy began to bark, his tail wagging madly, but Mrs Talbot held him firmly on his lead so that he couldn't run over.

Andi was relieved that Neil O'Connor had ridden away once she was back with the group – she would have hated her mum to see her being led along like a baby – though she was still fuming about the way he'd treated her.

"Normally our riders untack their own ponies, but I'll take Sunshine for you," Shona said. "I should think you've had enough for today."

"Thanks." Andi handed over the reins, glad

that she wouldn't have to take off Sunshine's saddle and bridle herself. She patted the pony. "Thanks, girl." She didn't blame Sunshine for what had happened.

Mrs O'Connor came out of her office with a man and a woman. "There!" the man said, pointing at Sunshine. "That one's perfect!"

"I'm sorry," Mrs O'Connor said. "I've already told you, I haven't got any ponies for sale."

"But it's for our son," the woman said indignantly. "And he's got his heart set on a buckskin just like that mare."

The man took out his cheque book. "How much? Come on, that pony's just what we want."

"I'm afraid I can't help you," Mrs O'Connor said.

"Well, thanks for nothing!" the man snapped. "Come along, Alicia." He marched to his car, climbed in and slammed the door. With a final furious glance at Sunshine, his wife followed him.

"Trouble?" Shona asked as the car roared away.

"Just some people who want to buy a buckskin pony for their son. I've given them the addresses of a couple of farms, but I don't think anyone's got a buckskin for sale at the moment." Mrs O'Connor shrugged. "Even if I had a pony for sale, I don't think I'd sell it to them after the way they behaved!"

Andi hugged Sunshine before she said goodbye. She was glad the pretty mare wasn't going to be sold to such a horrible couple.

"How did it go?" asked Mrs Talbot, when Andi ran across to her.

"Not great." Andi crouched down to pet Buddy and he squirmed on to her lap, overjoyed to see her again.

"Oh? What happened?"

Andi gently pushed Buddy off her lap and stood up. "I don't know. I suppose I just don't like riding much." There was no way she was going to tell her mum about horrible Neil O'Connor, who thought he was so great just because he knew everything about ducks and horses! She felt herself blushing just thinking about what had happened.

Mrs Talbot looked at her quizzically, but to Andi's relief she didn't say any more.

That evening, Andi's dad called. "Tell him I'm out," Andi whispered.

Her mum covered the mouthpiece of the

receiver. "No, Andi. He wants to know how your riding lesson went."

Andi pulled a face.

"Those lessons cost him a lot of money," Mrs Talbot went on. "Tell him you had a great time."

Andi could hardly believe her ears. Her mum had been dead set against the idea of her taking riding lessons, and now she wanted Andi to pretend that her first lesson had gone like something out of a Lassie movie – but with horses. She took the phone. "Hello, Dad."

"Hi, honey. How did your lesson go?"

"Well, the instructor is nice and the ponies are beautiful, but – oh, by the way, Mum says thanks for the seeds!"

"I'm glad she likes them. And I'm glad you like your instructor. I have some great news! I'm going to be in England next week for a meeting. I'll be able to come up to Aldcliffe to see you at the weekend. In fact, I thought I'd come see you ride."

Andi bit her lip. She'd have to go to the stables now – but it would be brilliant to see her dad again.

"I thought you might like to bring a friend along

to ride with you," he went on. "We can make a whole day of it – there must be some great places for lunch out in the mountains."

"Yeah. Thanks, Dad. I'll bring my friend Natalie. I told you about her before, remember? See you Saturday." Andi hung up, just hoping that Neil O'Connor wouldn't be round while she was having her lesson.

"Do you want to come riding with me on Saturday morning, Nat?" Andi asked next day after school. She and Natalie were waiting for Tristan in the school playground. He was in a different class to them and he often came out a few minutes late.

"Riding's not really my sort of thing." Natalie unzipped her rucksack and took out her new peach-flavoured lip-gloss. "Do you want to try some of this? It's heavenly!"

"No thanks."

Andi watched Natalie gloss her lips. "Please come, Nat," she begged. "It'll be really great!"

Natalie raised her eyebrows. "Well, if it's really that important . . ."

"What's important?" Tristan asked, running up.

Andi linked arms with Natalie. "We're going riding on Saturday."

Tristan frowned. "It's true then. It really *is* spreading," he said in a voice of doom.

"What is?" Andi and Natalie demanded at the same time.

"Riding disease," Tristan said in a whisper, glancing all round to check that nobody was listening. "The government's trying to hush it up, but news is starting to leak out. First one person catches it, then another, and before you know it just about everyone is heading for the stables dressed in ridiculous clothes."

Andi gave him a playful dig in the ribs. "Oh, that reminds me, my dad said I could have some chaps as an early Christmas present."

"Brilliant!" Natalie flipped her ponytail over her shoulder. "I've always wanted a pair of chaps! Suede is totally in this season. Let's go shopping after school tomorrow."

"Shame I can't come and watch you rodeo-riding on Saturday," Tristan said. "But I'm helping out at Paws for Thought." Paws for Thought was a pet shop owned by Christine Wilson, Tristan's mum's cousin. Christine often helped the Pet Finders by displaying posters or by giving them information about the type of animal they were searching for.

"Don't worry, Tris," Andi teased. "It'd be better to stay well away from Riverside Stables if you don't want to catch riding disease!"

Natalie pursed her lips and pretended to look thoughtful. "I don't know, Andi. He could look pretty cute in chaps and a ten-gallon hat!"

Next day after school, Andi and Natalie headed for the outdoor-clothing shop. "I looked up riding clothes on the Internet last night," Natalie said. "You should have seen some of those chaps. Seriously cool!"

"Are you buying some as well?" Andi asked.

"You bet!"

"But what if you don't like riding? You might decide not to go again."

"I don't want to wear the wrong thing. And chaps will be perfect."

Andi laughed. Natalie had more clothes than a department store! "So what colour do you want?" she said.

"I don't mind. Just as long as they're gorgeous."

Andi grinned. She was feeling more upbeat about her riding lessons again. They'd be in the sand school – the outdoor arena – this Saturday, and there wouldn't be any snakes there. And with any luck, Neil O'Connor would be out on the mountainside again. In fact, the more Andi thought about it, the more certain she was that Saturday would be great. Seeing her dad again would be terrific – and she'd have new chaps to wear, too!

They found the rail holding pairs of chaps. They were backless leather leggings held together with a belt that helped protect your legs from chafing after a long day in the saddle. Andi was astonished to see how many different designs there were. Some were plain leather or suede in shades of tan or brown; others were far more fancy, patterned or fringed in a range of colours.

Natalie seized a pair of heavily-fringed, scarlet chaps patterned with gold swirls. "These are amazing! What do you think, Andi?"

Before Andi had a chance to reply, Natalie spotted a pair of purple chaps decorated with pink zigzags. "Oh, these are even better!"

Andi stared at her in astonishment. "You're not serious?"

"I am. They're fantastic!" Natalie pulled them on. "Perfect!"

Shaking her head, and hoping she never ended up sharing Nat's fashion sense, Andi selected a pair of tan chaps patterned in a slightly darker brown. She buckled them on and looked approvingly at her reflection.

Natalie wrinkled her nose. "You're not going to buy *them*, are you?"

"What's wrong with them?"

"They're so plain and – oh, look at this!" Natalie darted across the shop and snatched up a suede jacket with fringed sleeves. "I must have this!" She pulled it on and twirled in front of the mirror, setting the fringes swinging.

"Are you sure?" Andi asked doubtfully. "It looks a bit Annie Oakley-ish. You don't think it's a bit over the top?"

"It'll be perfect for riding lessons." Natalie took off the chaps. "And I'll have these, too. Now, let's go and pay."

Draping the tan chaps over her arm, Andi

followed her to the counter, hoping Natalie's urban cowgirl look wouldn't raise too many eyebrows at Riverside. At this rate, she was going to scare the ducks even more than Buddy had!

Chapter Four

Andi woke early on Saturday morning. She was going to see her dad! She dragged on her clothes, keeping the chaps to put on at the stables, and ran downstairs with Buddy racing behind her.

"Mum, can I have my breakfast outside, so I can watch for Dad?"

"I don't see why not. He said he'd be here about nine o'clock, so you shouldn't have long to wait. He'll be in a rental car, don't forget."

"OK." Andi fed Buddy, grabbed her slice of toast and darted outside. She sat on the top step to eat.

The road was pretty quiet – it was too early for most of the neighbours to be out yet. Two cars passed, but both drivers were women. Then a blue car turned into Andi's road. As it came nearer, Andi spotted her dad in the driving seat. "Dad!" she yelled, racing down the steps and waving furiously.

Mr Talbot parked outside Andi's house and jumped out of the car. "Andi, how are you doing?"

Andi gave him a big hug. "I'm fine! Come and see Mum. And Buddy."

Buddy hurtled out of the living room to greet them, his tail wagging so fast that it was just a blur.

Mr Talbot crouched down to stroke him. "How are you, Bud? And how do you like living in Aldcliffe?"

"He loves it here," Andi told him.

Buddy barked as though agreeing with her, then began to race round Mr Talbot.

Andi's dad laughed, his dark eyes crinkling. "Calm down, Buddy! You'll make me dizzy."

Mrs Talbot came downstairs, carrying the vacuum cleaner. "Hello, David. Would you like a coffee?"

"Yes, please."

"Why don't you show your dad your bedroom, Andi, while I make the coffee?"

Andi led her dad up the two flights of stairs to

her attic bedroom. It was a quirky shape, with sloping ceilings and a window that gave a distant view of the mountains.

"This is great," her dad said enthusiastically. "I bet you can see the mountain-tops when you're in bed!"

"Only if it's not cloudy. And Aldcliffe gets more than its fair share of cloudy days, believe me!"

Mr Talbot laughed as he followed Andi downstairs again.

"Dad," Andi twisted round to look up at him, "you haven't asked about Pet Finders yet! We're not working on a case at the moment, but we're getting a pretty good reputation round Aldcliffe for finding missing pets."

Her dad raised his eyebrows. "Yes, from your emails I guessed there wasn't a cat or a rabbit that could leave home without being pounced on by one of you guys!"

Andi felt a prickle of annoyance that her dad didn't seem to be taking their pet-finding as seriously as they did, but before she could say anything, her mum appeared with a tray of hot drinks.

"Come into the living room," she invited.

Andi sat on the sofa next to her dad and sipped her hot chocolate. Her mum and dad chatted about work and about the problems of moving to a new town. Andi was relieved that they got on so well: she knew lots of people whose divorced parents started arguing the minute they saw each other.

"You ought to get going," Mrs Talbot said at last. "It takes half an hour to get to Riverside Stables and you've got to pick up Natalie on the way."

Buddy trotted into the hall behind them. "Sorry, Bud," Andi said. "You've got to stay with Mum today." She gave him a hug. "Make sure you're a good boy."

"As if he'd be anything else," Mr Talbot said, appearing in the living-room doorway. "Now let's go."

Andi darted outside, then stopped to watch her dad come down the steps. She was determined to make today a really great day: with her dad here as well, she was sure everything was going to be perfect!

* * *

Natalie ran out of her house as soon as Mr Talbot pulled up outside. She was dressed in her new riding gear, and Andi was startled to see just how bright her chaps were in daylight.

Beaming, Natalie slid into the back seat of the car beside Andi. "Hello, Andi. Is this your dad? Hello, Mr Talbot. Thanks for inviting me today."

"Hi, Natalie." Mr Talbot flashed her a smile in the driving mirror. "Are you all set?"

"You bet! What do you think of my outfit, Andi?"

Andi shrugged. Her plan to make everything perfect for her dad seemed to be crumbling already: Natalie looked as though she was a contestant for Cowgirl of the Year! "Those chaps are a bit bright," she said in a low voice. "And all those fringes!"

"What's wrong with them?" Natalie asked in an icy whisper.

"You look like Miss Rodeo!"

Natalie glowered at her. "I do not!" They were still whispering so Mr Talbot wouldn't hear.

"Couldn't you just have worn your ordinary jacket?" Andi blurted out. She knew she was making things worse, but she really wanted her dad to like

48

Natalie and not think she was some kind of fashion victim.

"I do know how to dress, Andi. And I happen to think that this outfit is perfect!" Natalie turned away pointedly and stared out of the window.

Andi wished she could take back what she'd said. She placed a hand on Natalie's arm, wanting to apologize, but Natalie shook her off. "Leave me alone."

Andi sat back. She'd say sorry later, when they reached the stables.

"You two are very quiet," Mr Talbot said, when they'd been driving for about a quarter of an hour.

"We're just thinking about our riding lesson," Natalie said. "Aren't we, Andi?"

"That's right." Andi forced a smile. "I can hardly wait."

"Great! I knew riding lessons would be the perfect present for you."

To Andi's dismay, Neil O'Connor was in the yard when they arrived. As if she needed things to get any worse! He watched them climb out of the car. "You decided to come back then, did you? Well, don't worry," he called. "You'll be perfectly safe this week because you're riding in the arena." He swung a head collar, the simple bitless bridle that could be used to lead horses round, over his shoulder and disappeared into a stable.

Andi felt her cheeks go bright red.

"What does he mean?" asked Mr Talbot.

"My pony was frightened by a snake last week." Andi could feel her face growing hotter by the second. "It wasn't anything really. I wonder which pony Natalie will get to ride?" She quickly changed the subject.

Natalie had gone on ahead and was leaning on the rail of the arena. Her back was very stiff and straight, and Andi knew she was still annoyed. She hurried over to her. "Nat, I'm really sorry I said that about your clothes."

Natalie looked round at her. "I suppose I might have overdone it a bit. Perhaps I should have steered clear of fringes." She smiled.

Andi smiled back. "Are we friends again?"

"Definitely." Natalie linked arms with her.

Mr Talbot came over. "It looks like everyone's waiting for you two."

"Right," Andi said, climbing through the rails into

the sandy-floored area. Natalie and Mr Talbot followed her. Tim, Helen and Darryl were there already, sitting on their ponies. Helen was chattering away to nobody in particular about how she wanted to be a famous showjumper when she grew up.

Mrs O'Connor was holding Sunshine and a brown pony with a black mane and tail that Andi hadn't seen before. She smiled. "Hello, Andi. And this must be your dad and Natalie." She and Mr Talbot shook hands. "I'm in charge of today's lesson. Shona's taken a party out on the mountain."

Natalie put on her riding hat. "Which pony am I riding?"

"Donna, the bay."

Natalie's face lit up. "I love her coat. She's so shiny, I might need to wear sunglasses!"

"Is Sara coming this week?" Andi asked.

"No, she doesn't actually live in Aldcliffe. She was just spending last weekend with her aunt. It was her aunt who arranged the ride for her."

Andi was pleased that Natalie was riding Donna, because it meant that she would get Sunshine again. She had really enjoyed riding her last week, in spite of the snake incident.

"Enjoy your lesson," Mr Talbot said. "I'll lean on the gate and watch."

"OK." Andi and Natalie mounted their ponies, then waited while Mrs O'Connor walked out to the centre of the arena to start the lesson.

"Welcome, everyone," she said, smiling round. She told them to walk round in a circle, using their legs and seat rather than their hands to guide their ponies. "Sit up straight, Tim," Mrs O'Connor called. "Don't hunch over the pony's neck like that. And hold the reins loosely with one hand. This is Western riding where we steer with our legs, not English where we use the reins more. Think of all those cowboy films!"

Andi soon found that she was enjoying the lesson and she was glad now that she'd had to come.

Suddenly she realized that Neil was sitting on the fence watching them. She sat up straighter in her saddle, determined to show him that she knew how to ride.

"Change to a trot now," Mrs O'Connor said. "You should post in time with your pony's stride. That means rise up out of the saddle: one, two, one, two. Up, down, up, down."

Andi gave Sunshine a kick and she broke into a trot. As she was passing Neil, she somehow missed Sunshine's stride and flopped down in the saddle like a fish just as Sunshine's back was rising. It was such a stupid mistake. She'd trotted loads of times before. Why did she have to mess it up this time, with her dad and Neil watching? Quickly, she corrected herself.

"You're doing well," Neil called.

Andi glanced over her shoulder in surprise, but he was talking to Natalie. Andi had to admit that she *was* riding well, rising and falling exactly in time with Donna's stride.

Natalie beamed back at Neil.

Great, Andi thought. *It looks as though my best friend's got a crush on my worst enemy!*

"Cantering, now," called Mrs O'Connor. "It's quicker than trotting so you'll need to shorten your reins a bit to keep control of your pony."

Andi urged Sunshine into a canter. Usually, she managed to lose a stirrup when she was cantering, but today she succeeded in keeping both feet in place.

"Great, everyone," Mrs O'Connor said, when

they had all completed a circuit. "That's it for today. Can you all untack your ponies, please? The saddles and bridles go in the tack room at the far end of the stable block." She pointed it out.

Andi slid down from Sunshine's back and patted her. "Good girl, Sunshine." It didn't take long to take off her saddle and bridle, then she made her way over to where her dad was waiting. He smiled broadly at her. "Good job, Andi. You looked great out there."

Before Andi could reply, Natalie came tearing across the yard with her riding hat under her arm. "Neil says he'll show us round the farm, Andi! Isn't that great?"

Andi's heart sank. She didn't want to find herself stuck with the Neil-and-Natalie mutual fan club. "There won't be time. We've got to get some lunch."

"Well, I'm in no hurry," Mr Talbot said. "I'd love to have a look round."

Neil came over. "Are you ready?"

Natalie ran her hands through her long blonde hair and tucked a wayward strand behind her ear. "You bet! I've always been interested in farms."

Andi gazed at her in disbelief. A farmyard was

the last place Natalie would choose to hang out! She was always so concerned about her designer clothes that she wouldn't want to be within a million miles of a muddy field! But even though she'd just been riding, she still looked cool and immaculate. Andi sighed. She was boiling hot and she knew her face would be red. There was a wet patch on her jumper, too, where Sunshine had dribbled on her.

"I'll show you the goats first." Neil led them to the barn. Mr Talbot stopped to talk to Shona, who had just ridden into the yard, while Andi trailed along behind Natalie and Neil feeling like a spare part.

"Oh, they're adorable!" Natalie exclaimed as they went into the barn.

The cute fluffy goat that Andi had stroked before was lying by the fence again. It stood up when it saw her and she leant over the rail to rub its head. To her amazement, Natalie started stroking the goats as well, and didn't even flinch when one of them nibbled the fringe on her jacket.

"Come and look at the duck pond now," Neil said, after a few minutes. "The ducks are mine."

"You lucky thing!" Natalie gasped. "I've always wanted to keep ducks."

Andi stared at her. "No you haven't!"

"Yes I have!" She grinned. "You don't know everything about me, Andi." Turning to Neil again, she said, "I'm really committed to animals. That's why I helped set up the Pet Finders Club with Andi and our friend, Tristan. You might have heard of it? We've investigated some really important cases of lost pets."

Neil looked at Andi as though he expected her to join in the conversation, but she pretended she hadn't noticed. There was no way she was going to make friends with Mr High-and-Mighty Neil O'Connor!

"It sounds like a great idea!" Neil said enthusiastically, turning to Natalie again. "Tell me about some of your cases."

"Oh, we've found loads of missing animals – cats, dogs, guinea pigs. Once we even tracked down some stolen lizards. We haven't had a case yet that we couldn't solve."

"Give me your phone number, then if anyone's lost a pet I can tell them who to contact," Neil said.

"Here you are." Natalie pulled out a handful of flyers advertising the Pet Finders Club. Normally the flyers carried Andi's phone number, but these had Natalie's on because Andi had dropped her phone and broken it on an early-morning run.

"These are amazing! Let's put them in my mum's office," Neil suggested. He and Natalie walked away.

Andi stayed where she was. She watched the ducks swimming round on the pond for a while, then went to find her dad. Hopefully he'd say it was time to go to lunch: Andi wanted to get away from Neil as soon as she possibly could!

The café Mr Talbot took Andi and Natalie to was cute, with red-and-white gingham curtains and tablecloths. They sat at the counter on seats made out of real saddles, and ate burgers and chips with banana milkshakes. While they waited for dessert, Mr Talbot chatted away about his coming trip to Malaysia to deal with some problems on an oil rig.

After lunch Mr Talbot dropped Natalie at her house, then took Andi home. "I won't come in," he said as he drew up outside. "I've got to get to the airport for that flight to Malaysia."

Andi hugged him. "Thanks for coming, Dad. It's been lovely to see you again."

"I'll send you a postcard."

"Thanks. And I'll get Mum to take some digital pictures of me riding, so I can email them to you."

"Great! I'll give you a call as soon as I get home."

Andi suddenly felt very lonely as she watched him drive away. It was really hard, only seeing him a few times a year. She loved living with her mum – and Buddy – but she missed her dad like mad. Especially now that they lived in different countries.

Chapter Five

As she went into the school playground on Monday morning, Andi looked round for Natalie and Tristan.

Natalie waved to her from behind a group of Year Fives. "Andi," she called. "Wow! Great weekend! You didn't tell me about Neil! He is so gorgeous."

Andi blinked. Natalie obviously had a major crush on him!

"Thanks for taking me riding with you," Natalie went on. "I'd never have met him if it wasn't for you."

Andi pulled a face. "You're not serious?"

"I am. He's terrific! You must let me come with you again next week," Natalie said. "I've asked my mum and dad and they say it'll be all right."

Andi wasn't sure what to say. She could hardly

say no, because riding with a friend would be fun, but she wasn't keen on the idea of watching Nat and Neil moon over each other. Especially when Neil probably thought she was a dork for letting Buddy off the lead and for missing Sunshine's stride when she was trotting.

Natalie clutched her arm. "I'm relying on you, Andi. I can't get to the stables if I don't get a lift from you. My stepdad plays golf every Saturday morning and my mum goes to her bridge club."

Andi relented. "OK. I'm sure my mum won't mind giving you a lift."

Natalie punched the air. "Yahoo! Thanks, Andi." She linked arms with her. "Now tell me everything you know about Neil. And don't you dare miss out a single thing."

The Pet Finders were in the playground on Thursday lunchtime, standing with their backs to the bitter wind, when Natalie's mobile phone rang. She looked down at the caller ID and her face brightened. "It's Neil!"

He must be really serious, thought Andi. Beside her, Tristan rolled his eyes. He was obviously getting a bit fed up with hearing about the amazing Neil O'Connor.

Natalie answered the phone with a cheery, "Hi there!", but quickly looked serious. "Neil, that's terrible!" She paused, listening. "Of course we'll help, but we won't be able to get there until Saturday. See you then." She snapped her phone shut and slipped it into her bag.

"What's happened?" Andi asked.

"One of the ponies has gone missing from the stables! Neil wants us to find her." Natalie slid an arm round Andi's shoulders. "I'm sorry, Andi. It's Sunshine."

Andi bit her lip. "Oh no! I wish we could go over to Riverside Stables right now."

"Not much chance of that," Tristan pointed out. "The bell's going to ring any minute now. It'll be quite a challenge, finding a pony," he added. "They may be bigger than your average dog or cat, but I reckon they could travel further."

"I can't believe Sunshine might be out on the mountainside, lost and alone," Andi sighed.

"She might not be on the mountain," Natalie said. "Neil says she could have been stolen."

"Stolen!" Andi stared at Natalie in horror. "That's even worse!"

"Well, we're the right people to tackle the case," Tristan said. "We've got a great track record with solving crimes. Though I suppose we should try not to get too close to any thieves." He was clearly remembering the trouble they had got into over the reptile thief that raided Christine's shop.

"The police are investigating," Natalie continued, "but they haven't found her yet."

"Poor Sunshine," Andi said sadly. "Oh, I hope we can get her back."

Andi was up extra-early on Saturday morning, though she'd stayed up late the night before checking the Internet for articles about horse thieves. She rushed downstairs to help with the chores so that she and her mum could leave for the stables as soon as possible.

Mr Peterson dropped Natalie at Andi's house just before nine o'clock. "Don't come in," Andi warned, as she opened the door. "We're leaving straightaway." She clipped on Buddy's lead and called to her mum.

"Hurry up!" Natalie exclaimed impatiently. "I can't wait to get to the stables." She was wearing a denim jacket, with blue jeans tucked into suede boots, and a lilac hairband.

Mrs Talbot came hurrying downstairs. "I'm all ready. Let's go."

Andi and Natalie sprinted to the car and dived into the back seat; Buddy leapt in after them. "Isn't Tristan coming with you?" Mrs Talbot asked, as she reversed out of the drive.

"He's helping out at Paws for Thought today," Natalie replied. "But he's given me a huge list of things to find out about while we're at the stables."

"Did you phone Mrs O'Connor, Andi, to cancel your riding lesson?"

"Yes. I told her we'd like to help find Sunshine. She said the police can't work out where she might be or who might have taken her. It's a real puzzle."

"We'll crack it," Natalie said confidently. "We haven't been beaten yet."

The journey to the stables seemed to take for ever. "I hope we can find her," Andi said for the millionth time as they passed the sign for Riverside Stables.

Neil ran out to meet them when they drove into the stable yard. He was wearing a battered yard coat and muddy jeans over sturdy Wellington boots. "Thanks for coming," he said. "I'll tell you what happened while I feed the goats."

"What time shall I come and get you?" asked Mrs Talbot, as Andi and Natalie scrambled out of the car.

"It's okay, Mum, we can catch the bus. Natalie found out that one runs from the end of the drive all the way back to Aldcliffe. It stops outside Rocky's shop."

"That's handy," Mrs Talbot said. "And not having to drive all the way out here again will give me the chance to take Buddy for a walk. That way you won't have to rush home."

Andi beamed at her, appreciating the way her mum took pet-finding as seriously as they did. "Thanks, Mum."

"Don't leave the farm, though, okay? And don't get in the way. Mrs O'Connor's still got a business to run here."

"Okay. See you later, Mum. And you, Buddy." Andi patted Buddy, gave her mum a quick kiss and darted after Natalie and Neil, who were heading for the barn.

"Sunshine was in the far paddock with some other ponies when she disappeared," Neil began. He stopped at a tiny storeroom containing bags of animal food and hoisted out a bag of flaked grain. "The goats need extra food at this time of year because there's not enough grass for them," he explained. He led the way into the barn, tossed the bag of feed over the barrier and climbed after it. The black-and-white goats milled about him, bleating excitedly. "All right, you greedy lot." He threaded his way between them, tucking the bag under one arm and ripping it open with his free hand. "I'm going as fast as I can."

"Which other ponies were in the paddock with Sunshine?" Natalie asked.

"Bonnie, Chipper, Donna and Scrumpy." Neil tipped food into the first trough. The goats gathered round, nudging each other aside in their determination to eat first.

"And my horse, Flash. Oh, and Tilly. But the thief only took Sunshine."

"The thief left Flash and Tilly?" Andi checked, puzzled.

"I know. Those two were much more valuable than Sunshine." Neil glanced round at her, shaking his head as if he couldn't understand it either, then headed for another trough with a line of goats skittering behind him. "The police thought it was weird, too. They wondered if the thief had been disturbed, but we didn't hear the dogs barking or the ducks quacking."

Natalie looked at him in surprise. "Ducks?"

"Ducks and geese make great watchdogs. They're very suspicious of strangers and can set up a real racket if they don't like the look of someone. But not in this case."

"When did you find out Sunshine was missing?" Natalie questioned.

"On Thursday morning. We often leave the horses and ponies out overnight if it's not too cold. There's a really solid field shelter in that paddock. The horses can go right inside, and they all wear blankets at night at this time of year, anyway." He filled the last trough and trudged back. "They don't like being cooped up in the stable much, but we've been bringing them in at about four o'clock since Sunshine disappeared."

"Can we have a look at the paddock?" Andi said.

"I'll take you up there now."

Andi and Natalie followed him outside and along the narrow pathway that ran between the side of the barn and the stables. Andi felt her cheeks go red as they passed the duck pond, remembering how Buddy had chased the ducks just before she first met Neil. He seemed different today, she thought, a bit quieter and less sure of himself. And he obviously really cared about his animals.

"We've got to go across the cow field to reach the far paddock," Neil warned. "Are you both okay with cows?"

"I am," Andi told him.

Natalie was walking beside Neil, but she glanced back at Andi and pulled a horrified face. Andi bit her lip, trying not to giggle.

Neil didn't notice. "*You* must like cows, Natalie," he said. "You seem to love anything to do with farming."

"What? Oh yes. I love them," Natalie replied hurriedly. "They're so – um, cute."

"Cute? Well, I suppose you could call them that."

"Actually, I like milk in shakes rather than on the hoof!" Natalie joked.

Neil gave her an odd look, then opened the gate.

Natalie stayed close to him as they crossed the field, but the cows took little notice of them; they just went on contentedly munching grass.

They reached the far side of the field and let themselves into the paddock through a five-barred gate. Andi looked round, trying to take in everything. *If only Tristan was here*, she thought. With his amazing memory, they wouldn't miss a single detail.

In the middle of the paddock stood a sturdy stone barn with a narrow doorway just wide enough to let a horse through. Two ponies, Tilly and Scrumpy, were cropping the grass on the sheltered side of the barn. Three more ponies and Neil's palomino, Flash, were standing in a huddle a little way off. The paddock had a wooden post-and-rail fence on three sides, with two gates – the one they'd just come through and another opening out on to the mountainside. Andi made a mental note to check that there were no loose rails that might have let Sunshine out. The river ran along

the fourth side of the paddock.

Natalie hung back to speak to Andi as Neil headed towards the barn. She took out Tristan's list and read the first item. "He wants us to look for tyre tracks. Could a thief have brought a lorry up here, do you think?"

"The gates are wide enough. And if he cut across the fields instead of driving through the stable yard, it would explain why Neil and his mum didn't hear anything."

"Let's go and check the gates, then."

"It's a shame Tris couldn't come," Andi said as they jogged back to the first gate. "He's really good at spotting things."

"You're right, but don't say that when he's around," Natalie warned with a grin. "He'll only get big-headed."

The ground round the gateway was soft and a bit muddy in places; there were plenty of hoofprints, but no tyre tracks. "Some of these hoofprints are probably Sunshine's," Andi said. "But how can we tell?"

Natalie shrugged. "I don't know, but I'm beginning to see why Neil wears old clothes. My jeans are muddy already and we've only been here a few minutes. I am *so* going to need a bath when I get home – and a washing machine!"

Andi laughed. "You and your clothes, Nat! Let's go and check the other gate." As she raced away, a fine drizzle began to fall.

"Hang on, Andi," Natalie called.

"What is it? Have you found something?" Andi spun round and ran back.

"No. But there doesn't seem much point both of us getting wet. Maybe someone should go and examine the barn."

Andi raised her eyebrows. "And you're volunteering, I bet."

"Somebody has to do it."

"Go on, then. I'll meet you in there." Andi pulled up her hood, then sped away.

There were no tyre tracks by the gate that led on to the mountain, either. Andi didn't know whether to be disappointed or relieved: if Sunshine had been taken away in a lorry, then she could be pretty well anywhere by now – maybe even in another county. But if she'd got away on foot, she could be lost on the mountain, with all those places where she could hurt herself or get stuck. Andi stared up at the pine forests stretching away, suddenly afraid that if Sunshine was somewhere in there, she might never be found.

Chapter Six

Andi blinked her eyes against the rain, wishing that
when she opened them again, she would see the
pretty buckskin trotting down the mountainside
towards her. But there was no sign of any animals at
all, apart from a speck in the sky that might have
been a circling hawk.

"Don't worry, Sunshine," she whispered,
determined not to be downhearted. "We'll find
you." But she couldn't help wondering how, when
they didn't have a single clue so far.

She checked the gate. The latch was well-oiled
and held fast even when Andi threw all her weight
against it. She tested the hinges, too, wondering if
Sunshine might have pushed her way out – the Pet
Finders had once tracked down a cat that had

escaped through a door with a broken hinge. But the metal fittings weren't damaged in any way and the gate swung firmly round its post.

Sighing, Andi jogged down to the barn, where she found Natalie making notes on the back of a receipt. "So what was the exact time when you found the ponies gone?" she asked Neil, sounding like a police detective – or Tristan.

"Just before half past seven in the morning."

Natalie scribbled this down. "Oh hello, Andi. Any luck?"

"No."

Natalie pulled a face, then returned to her questions. "Did you see anything unusual? Were either of the gates open maybe?"

"No, nothing. Everything was exactly the same as it always is, except that Sunshine wasn't here. Shona saw something though, when she was on her way into work on Thursday morning. She passed a big green horsebox. She said it was belting along, and she had to swerve to avoid it."

"Did she make a note of the number plate?" Andi asked eagerly.

"No. She didn't know Sunshine was missing

then, so it didn't seem important. But she noticed that it had a huge dent in the wing, with a big scrape of red paint on it."

Natalie wrote down the details. "I bet Sunshine was inside that lorry, and the thief was trying to make a quick getaway!"

"It certainly sounds suspicious," Andi agreed. "And a horsebox like that should be pretty easy to recognize – as long as they don't get the dent fixed, anyway." At least it would give them something to work on, she thought. Perhaps they could visit all the farms around Aldcliffe and see if anyone had a dented green horsebox.

"The police thought it might have been the thief, too," Neil said. "They said they'd keep an eye out for it."

"So what do we do now?" Natalie asked. "Start searching for the horsebox?"

"Not yet," Andi replied. "We don't know for sure that Sunshine was inside. Let's finish off here first. We ought to examine the fence. Maybe there's a break in it somewhere and the rail sort of bounced back in place after Sunshine had escaped."

Neil's eyebrows shot up, almost disappearing under his fringe. "I'm sure we'd have noticed if there was something wrong with the fence."

"It's got to be worth checking, though," Andi insisted.

Natalie looked out through the open doorway. "It's raining harder now." She wrinkled her nose. "I don't want to smudge my notes. Tris would never forgive me."

"Put them in your pocket," Andi said. "That'll keep them dry." She moved close to Natalie and lowered her voice. "You don't want Neil thinking you're scared of a bit of rain, do you?" she teased.

Natalie gave an indignant sniff, then stuffed the receipt in her pocket. "I suppose we *should* check the fence." Turning up her collar, she followed Andi outside.

They walked slowly round the edge of the paddock, checking the fence for signs of damage. Here and there, where the rails were rough and a bit splintery, they found a few strands of coarse pony hair in various colours.

"This looks like Sunshine's hair," Natalie said excitedly, gathering a few yellow strands.

"That doesn't mean anything," Neil warned. "The ponies often stand against the fence. Their hair just gets snagged."

"I'll keep it anyway. We might need to match it against another clump of hair later on in the investigation." Natalie placed the hair carefully in her pocket. "We had to do that once before, for a puppy we found."

"What about the river?" Andi said. "Could Sunshine have waded across?"

"It's way too deep," Neil said.

All the same, they went to have a closer look. As Neil had said, it was very deep – and fast flowing, too.

"You don't think she could have fallen in?" Andi asked with a shiver. No animal would have stood a chance in that swift current.

"No! Sunshine's really surefooted," Neil said. "In any case, the horses don't need to go to the river even if they're thirsty. There's a water trough just outside the barn door."

Andi walked along the riverbank, while Natalie stood near the fence with Neil and drew a plan of the paddock on the back of Tristan's list. She held the paper close to her chest to shield it from the rain. To Andi's relief, there were no hoofprints anywhere near the water: Neil was obviously right about the horses keeping well away. But if it was so hard for the ponies to get out of the paddock on their own, it was looking more and more likely that Sunshine had been stolen. And if the green horsebox hadn't come from a local farm, she could be anywhere!

"Well, that's that," Natalie said, when Andi returned. She folded the plan and tucked it inside her jacket. "We've only got one clue. I really hope it turns out to be a good one because otherwise . . ." She shrugged.

Neil gulped. "You don't think you're going to find her, do you?" He turned away to fiddle with a splinter on the fence. "I'm so worried about her."

"We'll do our best," Andi said gently, squeezing his arm. Neil might be sharp with people, but he clearly cared a lot about animals.

He nodded and rubbed his eyes with his sleeve, then glanced at his watch. "I promised Mum I'd take some of the ponies back to the yard for her. Have you finished here?"

"Yep." Natalie put away her pen and shook raindrops from her hair.

"I'll fetch the ponies then." Neil vanished into the barn, reappearing a moment later with three rope halters. He delved into his pocket and brought out a chunk of carrot. Holding it on the flat of his hand, he walked towards Tilly and Scrumpy. They watched him approach, then Scrumpy trotted over, her ears pricked eagerly.

Neil rubbed her nose. "I can always rely on you, Scrumpy." He glanced over his shoulder at Andi and Natalie. "She's mad about carrots."

Andi thought about Sunshine. She hoped whoever had taken her was feeding her well.

Scrumpy took the carrot and, while she was chewing, Neil slipped the halter over her head. "Natalie, can you hang on to Scrumpy? I'll catch the others."

It took Neil only a few moments to slip the remaining two halters on to Tilly and Chipper. "Here, Andi." Neil handed her Tilly's halter rope, and they led the three ponies across the paddock to the gate.

As they crossed the cow field, Andi noticed a

smear of mud on Tilly's neck. She brushed it away. Underneath the mud there was a triangle of white hair with an R inside that stood out against the pony's chestnut coat. "Oh, Tilly's freeze branded!"

Andi glanced at Scrumpy and Chipper; they weren't quite as muddy, and neither of them seemed to have a brand. "How come Tilly's branded but these other two aren't?"

"Most of our horses are branded," Neil replied. "But we haven't had Scrumpy or Chipper long. We're waiting for someone to come and do it."

"What about Sunshine? Is she branded?"

"Yes."

Andi's heart began to beat faster. "But that doesn't make sense. Why didn't the thief take an unbranded horse that couldn't be traced?"

"I know. It's weird," Neil agreed. "And in any case, most thieves would take all the horses in one field at the same time. If you're only going to take one, why take one that's branded?"

Natalie peered closer at Tilly's brand. "How does it work?"

"Every horse owner has an iron cut in their own style of brand," Neil explained. "It's frozen on to the horse's skin and it makes the hair grow back differently. It's usually a different colour, and the texture of the hair changes, too."

Natalie shuddered. "It sounds horrible!"

"No, it doesn't really hurt. People say it's no worse than having your ears pierced."

"So when someone tries to sell the horse, buyers can check that it hasn't been stolen?" Natalie checked. She touched Tilly's brand gingerly as though she was afraid of hurting her.

Neil nodded. "There's a national register of brands. It makes selling a stolen horse with a brand pretty tricky."

"This could be a really important clue." Natalie gripped Andi's arm. "We must be looking for an inexperienced thief who doesn't know much about horses."

"Or someone who only ever steals one horse at a time," Andi said. "Like someone who works by themselves, or only has a small horsebox."

Natalie looked doubtful.

"Well, it's possible!" Andi said defensively.

"Perhaps we could look through some horse magazines," Natalie suggested. "We could read up on past thefts to see if there are any similarities with this case."

"I think Mum's got a whole stack in the office," Neil offered.

So, as soon as the ponies were handed over to their riders, Andi, Natalie and Neil hurried to Mrs O'Connor's office. It was a small, homely room with walls crammed with photos of horses and riders.

Andi and Natalie sat on a lumpy sofa to one side of the desk, while Neil opened the bottom drawer of the filing cabinet. "You Pet Finders really seem to know what you're doing," he said, taking out a pile of magazines. "This is a million times better than sitting around feeling helpless!"

He put the magazines on the sofa between Andi and Natalie, then perched on the desk. They began to leaf through them, starting with the most recent, but nearly all the reports of thefts referred to all the horses and ponies in one paddock being taken at the same time.

"How could they take them all?" Natalie asked. "Wouldn't the thieves need a whole fleet of horseboxes?"

"No. Not if they didn't mind cramming them in,"

Neil said. "Some of those big lorries would hold about twelve horses if they were squashed together. And you wouldn't get more than that in an average paddock."

They went on reading, but the only individual horses that had been stolen were famous showjumpers.

"Perhaps some horses get stolen to order," Natalie suggested, looking up from her magazine. "You know, like paintings."

Andi and Neil stared at her blankly.

"If a crooked art collector wants a particular painting, they can pay someone to steal it," Natalie went on. "Then they hang it in their private collection and nobody knows where it's gone. Perhaps it's the same with horses. People could steal top-class horses and breed from them, even if they had to keep the stolen horse secret."

"That doesn't explain why anyone would take Sunshine," Andi pointed out. "She's a lovely pony, but she's not famous or really well-bred."

"I suppose whoever took her might have wanted an ordinary riding pony," Neil said. "But then why didn't they take an unbranded pony?"

Natalie shrugged. "Perhaps Sunshine was the easiest to catch."

They went on scouring the magazines for another half an hour. "This is hopeless!" Andi said at last. She straightened up, rubbing her back. "I don't suppose you've got a photo of Sunshine, have you, Neil?"

"Yes. Here." He took one down from the wall next to the window and handed it to her. The pretty buckskin mare was standing in the stable yard, looking straight at the camera with her ears pricked.

"Hang about!" Andi exclaimed. "What about that couple who wanted a buckskin pony for their son?"

Neil and Natalie looked at her blankly.

"Didn't your mum mention them, Neil? They were here on the day of my first lesson." Andi felt herself blushing as she remembered the way Neil had rescued her when Sunshine bolted. "I've only just remembered. They were pretty huffy when your mum said Sunshine wasn't for sale." She stood up. "Let's go and talk to her about them."

They found Mrs O'Connor in the tack room,

cleaning a saddle. "Can you tell us anything about that rude couple who wanted to buy Sunshine?" Andi asked.

"We think they might have stolen her," Natalie added.

Mrs O'Connor frowned. "Oh, I don't know. They wouldn't steal her, surely?" She paused. "But they *were* very insistent. I ought to mention them to the police."

"Do you know their names?" Neil said. "Or where they live?"

His mother shook her head. "No. I don't really know anything about them. Except that they've got a son who wants a buckskin pony. And their car's some kind of big four-wheel drive."

"It was blue," Andi said. She thought hard, trying to recall more details, but she'd been so upset about her disastrous riding lesson that she hadn't paid much attention. "I don't know what make their car was. They were both tall, but I can't even think what colour hair they had or what they were wearing. Oh, this is hopeless – there must be loads of tall people with blue four-wheel drive cars!"

"Sorry I can't be more help," Mrs O'Connor said.

She put down her cleaning cloth. "I'll go and phone the police."

Andi, Natalie and Neil trailed back to the office and delved into the horse magazines again.

"We should go," Natalie said after about quarter of an hour, looking at her watch. "Otherwise we'll miss the bus."

"OK." Andi stood up. As she slipped on her coat, a headline in one of the magazines that was open on the table caught her eye.

RIDERS LEFT HORSELESS AFTER THEFT FROM LIVERY STABLES, it read. Andi picked up the magazine. There was a photo of some kids standing in an empty field, looking miserable. Andi scanned the article; all the ponies had been stolen in a night raid on the stables. She glanced at the photo again and gasped in astonishment.

"Look at this!" She waved the magazine under Natalie's nose. "I recognize one of the girls in this photo. It's Sara!"

Chapter Seven

"I met Sara when I came for my first lesson here," Andi explained. "Maybe she can give us a few tips about finding stolen ponies! She might have got her pony back in the end. Have you got her address, Neil?"

"Well, she was staying with her aunt when she came here." Neil opened the filing cabinet and took out a large book. He flipped through the pages until he found what he was looking for. "Here it is. Her aunt's called Mrs Walker. She lives at Halfpenny Farm, off Boundary Road in Aldcliffe."

"I know where that is," Andi said. "Tris and I went down that way with his dad a couple of weeks ago to take photos of a house he was selling. We can go over on our bikes, Nat, and ask for Sara's phone number."

"Good idea," Natalie agreed. "Isn't it weird how it's harder to find a big animal like a horse than a tiny little guinea pig? I mean, you'd have thought it would be impossible for a full-size horse to disappear!"

"You *are* going to stick with it, aren't you?" Neil asked anxiously.

"Of course we are. We'll do everything we can."

Andi heard a note of uncertainty in Natalie's voice and realized that she was starting to feel daunted. "We've never failed with a case yet," she said, trying to reassure her. "And we're not going to start now."

"Thanks," Neil said. "I'm really grateful."

Natalie glanced at her watch and gave a squeal. "Come on!" She yanked Andi to her feet. "Bye, Neil. I'll phone you as soon as we get any news."

"Let us know if you hear anything," Andi called over her shoulder, as Natalie bundled her out of the door.

As soon as they got back to Aldcliffe, Andi and Natalie collected their bikes and cycled to

Halfpenny Farm. It was on the very edge of Aldcliffe, not too far from Andi's house. The farmhouse, an old half-timbered building, was set back from the road at the end of a long driveway that ran between fields of apple trees. The trees were almost bare now, and fallen leaves and a few windfalls littered the ground beneath them.

"Those apples are making me feel thirsty," Andi said. "A glass of juice would be fantastic after that bike ride." She looked round. "I came here when I lost Buddy. I thought he might have run in among the trees and I called for ages, but there was no sign of him."

She and Natalie leant their bikes against the side of the house. "I hope someone's in after all that cycling," Natalie puffed.

Andi laughed. "Exercise is good for you, Nat."

"It might be good for *you*, but sitting around suits *me* just fine, thanks."

As they headed for the front door, it opened and a tall grey-haired woman stepped out carrying a suitcase. She stopped dead when she saw Andi and Natalie. "Can I help you?"

"We were hoping you could give us Sara's phone number," Andi said. "You are Mrs Walker, aren't you?"

The woman dropped her suitcase. "You know Sara?" she gasped.

"Not very well," Andi admitted, puzzled by the woman's reaction. "We went riding together at Riverside Stables."

Mrs Walker sighed and picked up her case again.

"Is something wrong?" Natalie asked.

Mrs Walker looked very grave. "I'm sorry to tell you this, but Sara went missing three days ago. Someone saw her waiting at a bus stop near her home, so she could be pretty well anywhere by now."

"You mean, she's run away?" Andi exclaimed in dismay.

"It looks like it. I'm off to stay with my sister's family now. I would have gone sooner, but I had to wait until my husband got back from a delivery trip. What did you want to speak to Sara about?"

"We're trying to find a stolen pony," Natalie explained. "We knew Sara's pony was stolen last year and we thought she might be able to give us some tips to help us find this one."

"It's not important now though," Andi added quickly. "Don't let us hold you up."

"No. I'd best get going. I want to get there before dark." Mrs Walker headed for a pickup truck that was parked to one side of the farmhouse. She put her suitcase on the passenger seat, then turned to Andi and Natalie again. "I think Sara went to lots of horse sales to try to get her pony back. Maybe you could try that." She climbed into the pickup and drove away.

"How awful!" Natalie said, wide-eyed. "Missing pets are one thing, but missing people . . . That's really serious! Why do you think she's run away?"

"I don't know, but I hope she's okay." Andi bit her lip. Usually that was what she thought about missing animals – somehow it seemed even scarier to be saying it about a person.

On Sunday morning, Natalie phoned Andi soon after breakfast. "Guess what? There's a horse sale on the other side of town today. My mum says she'll give us a lift there."

"OK," said Andi. "I've been thinking about Sara too, wondering if we can do anything to help find her, but I haven't come up with any ideas."

"Me neither. But the police and her family must be searching for her. If they can't find her, I don't see how we can be much use. So I think we might as well keep looking for Sunshine. This sale could be just the place."

"Yeah, you're right." What Natalie said made a lot of sense: they hadn't got the slightest idea where Sara might have gone, so how could they hope to help? "We'll stick to finding Sunshine and hope Sara turns up soon."

Mrs Talbot came into the hall. "Is there some news about Sunshine?"

"Hang on a sec, Nat." Andi quickly told her mum about the sale. "Is it OK to go?"

"Of course. Just make sure you're home in time to take Buddy for a walk."

Buddy seemed to sense Andi's excitement as she hurried to get ready. He raced round her, giving little high-pitched barks. "I'm sorry, Bud. I can't take you with me." Through the window, Andi saw Natalie's mum pull up outside. She gave Buddy a quick hug, then ran to put on her coat. "Bye, Mum. See you later." She darted out to the car, leaving

Buddy watching her mournfully from the living-room window.

The horse sale was bustling with people. Andi looked at the excited faces round her and thought how strange it was that she and Natalie were here for a totally negative reason: to find a pony that might have been stolen.

"Let's start over there," Natalie suggested, grabbing Andi's arm and steering her through the crowd. A bunch of little kids were clustered round the first pen, admiring a tiny Shetland pony. Andi wished they could stop – it looked so cute – but they didn't have time. Natalie's mum was reading a magazine in the car and Andi didn't want to make her wait for ages.

They squeezed through the crush to the next pen. A pair of enormous chestnut horses stood here, restlessly pawing the ground. "Keep going," Natalie urged. "It looks like there's a clearing up ahead."

They passed more horses and ponies but to Andi's disappointment, none of them looked like Sunshine.

Soon they reached a wide fenced-off space.

"This must be the auction arena," Andi said. She stood on tiptoe to see over the barrier. There were several ponies in the collecting ring on the far side, waiting to be sold. As she watched, they shifted and she saw a flash of copper-coloured hair. "Over there!" she exclaimed. "I'm sure one of those ponies is a buckskin." She grabbed Natalie's hand and dragged her between two men who were talking in loud voices about the price of a quarter-horse colt.

"What's a quarter-horse?" Natalie asked. "That seems an odd name, like it has just one leg or something!"

"It's a breed of horse that can run quarter of a mile really fast," Andi explained.

"Wow! I didn't know you knew stuff like that," Natalie said, clearly impressed.

Andi grinned. "I read it yesterday in one of Neil's horse magazines."

They wriggled through the crowd round the edge of the auction area, but when they reached the collecting ring, they could see that the buckskin was barely thirteen hands high. "That's not her," Andi said, disappointed. "Sunshine's closer to fourteen hands."

"There are a couple more buckskins down here," Natalie said. "Come on."

As they made their way along beside the pens, Andi saw the couple who'd tried to buy Sunshine from Mrs O'Connor. "It's them," she gasped. "The people who wanted Sunshine. Quick, let's follow them!"

"Do you think they've brought her here to sell her?" Natalie asked as they squeezed through the crowd, trying to keep them in sight. "Maybe they were lying when they said they wanted to buy her for their son. Or maybe he didn't like her after all."

The couple stopped by a pen containing a pair of buckskin ponies; neither of them was Sunshine. Andi and Natalie moved closer, wanting to hear what they said. "How much are they?" the woman asked.

Andi couldn't hear the owner's reply, but the man took out his cheque book immediately. "We'll take the one on the right," he said. "Our son will love it."

"They're not selling," Natalie sighed. "What a pain! I really thought we were on to something then. But it looks as if they really are buying a pony for their son."

Suddenly Andi heard someone calling her name. Glancing round, she saw Neil and Mrs O'Connor hurrying towards them. "It looks as though you had the same idea as us," said Mrs O'Connor.

"Have you found Sunshine yet?" Natalie asked.

"Not yet," Neil replied. "But there are loads of buckskins here. Maybe we'll strike it lucky. Did you speak to Sara?"

"No. She's run away," Andi said.

"Run away?" Neil echoed, shocked.

"That's terrible!" Mrs O'Connor exclaimed. "I hope they find her soon. What made her do it, I wonder?"

"Maybe she had a row with her parents or something," Natalie said. "Anyway, we ought to get searching for Sunshine in case somebody buys her."

Andi told Neil and his mum about the couple who'd wanted to buy Sunshine as they worked their way along the pens, stopping at every buckskin and looking them over carefully. Quite a few of them resembled Sunshine at first, but when they looked more closely they found that they were just too tall or too short, or a fraction too stocky or too thin. And none of them had a dark streak in their tail.

"She's not here," Andi said at last. "We've looked in every single pen."

"It was a long shot," Mrs O'Connor admitted. "Even if the thieves do plan to sell Sunshine on, they'll probably wait until people have stopped looking for her. She might not appear in a sale for months."

Andi looked at Neil's tense unhappy face and a wave of sympathy washed over her. She'd been heartbroken when she'd lost Buddy, so she knew exactly how he felt.

"Thanks for trying," Mrs O'Connor said. "Neil told me about your Pet Finders Club and I really appreciate the effort you're making to find Sunshine." She sighed. "I'm not sure we're going to get her back, though. It's beginning to look like she's vanished into thin air."

Andi's school was closed on Monday for staff training, so she and Natalie caught the bus to Riverside Stables. Buddy went with them, firmly clipped to his lead. They planned to go up the mountain this time in the hope that Sunshine had somehow got out of the paddock on her own, and Andi knew Buddy would enjoy the walk.

"It's a shame Tristan couldn't come," Natalie said, as they got off the bus outside the stables. He'd promised to help Christine with a big delivery of feed at the pet shop. "What with him helping out at Paws for Thought, and going skateboarding all the time, we've hardly seen him lately."

"We'll ring him if we find anything," Andi promised.

Neil was mucking out the stables when they reached the yard. "Hello," Natalie called.

He whirled round, nearly stabbing himself in the foot with his pitchfork. "Have you found her?"

"Not yet. We're going to look for her on the mountain. What are you doing here anyway? We thought you'd be at school today."

"Staff training. Is that why you're off, too?"

"Yes."

Neil grinned. "They should have training days more often. I'd much rather be here than at school." He glanced at his watch. "If you can hang on for twenty minutes, I'll come with you. I've got a few chores to finish first."

"We could give you a hand," Andi suggested. "It'll be quicker if we all help."

"Great! I'll fetch a couple of brooms." Neil disappeared into the stable.

"Thanks, Andi," Natalie said sarcastically. "I've always wanted to muck out a stable. Not!"

"Sorry. But it would be good if Neil came too. It's getting quite cloudy and I don't like the idea of being out on the mountain when it's bucketing down with rain."

Natalie took off her coat. "I'm not going to risk getting this dirty. I've only had it a couple of weeks." She draped it over the lower half of the stable door.

Andi gaped at her. "What on earth are you wearing?"

"Dungarees."

Andi stared. Natalie was always buying clothes – it was surprising to see her dressed in anything that was more than a month old – but these dungarees looked ancient. Made of faded denim, they were patched and worn and the buttons didn't match.

"Where did you get them?"

"They're my mum's."

Now Andi was even more astonished. She had never seen Natalie's mum, who was a successful interior designer, wear anything but gorgeous designer clothes.

Natalie saw the look of disbelief on Andi's face. "Mum thinks she might have to pitch in with the painting one day if a decorator lets her down." She grinned. "There's not much chance of that, though, if you ask me. She knows hundreds of painters. Do you think I've overdone the whole country look?" Natalie suddenly looked anxious.

"Well, you certainly look different," Andi admitted.

"But is it too much?"

Before Andi had a chance to reply, Neil reappeared carrying two brooms. He handed one to Natalie and the other to Andi.

"We need to sweep the last of the straw out of the stable, and then put in some fresh stuff. You can tie Buddy's lead to this hook, Andi. That should keep him out of mischief."

"He's not going to get up to mischief today," Andi promised, ruffling Buddy's ears. "You're going to be a really good boy, aren't you, Bud?"

"I'll believe that when I see it," Neil muttered darkly.

Andi felt a flash of irritation. *Trust Neil to say a thing like that!* She wrapped the end of Buddy's lead round the hook, and he flopped down to watch what she was doing.

It didn't take long to sweep the stable. Neil fetched a bale of straw and cut the string so that they could spread it across the floor. By the time they'd finished, Natalie had bits of straw sticking out of her hair. Andi began to suspect that she'd be putting her name down for the Young Farmers' Club – she certainly looked the part – although she couldn't imagine Mr and Mrs Peterson being too pleased about having a batch of ducklings swimming in their pool!

"Andi, could you fetch a rug from the storeroom at the end of the barn?" Neil said. "I think Badger needs an extra layer. He's our oldest horse and he really feels the cold."

The storeroom was crammed full, reminding Andi of her wardrobe crossed with an outdoor supplies store. The floor was hidden beneath a stack of buckets, a roll of chicken wire, and a variety of spades, brooms, pitchforks and other tools that Andi didn't recognize. At the far end, shelves reached from floor to ceiling. They were crowded with pieces of tack, cleaning cloths, grooming brushes and an assortment of boxes containing who-knew-what. Andi raised her eyebrows. And she thought Buddy needed a lot of accessories!

She searched around, but she couldn't find any rugs. She went back to the stable. "Sorry, Neil, but I can't find it."

He tutted. "It's on one of the shelves. I don't know how you missed it."

Andi shrugged. She was doing her best: it wasn't *her* fault if things weren't where he thought they should be. "You'll have to find it yourself." She followed him as he went to look for the missing rug.

He flung open the storeroom door. "It's right here, on the . . ." The words died on his lips. "Oh! Where's it gone?"

"I'm off now, Neil. See you tomorrow," said a deep voice.

Andi whirled round. A tall man in his mid-forties, with dark curly hair flecked with grey, was crossing the yard with a rather rusty bike.

"Ted, you haven't seen Badger's rug, have you?" Neil asked.

"No, sorry." Ted climbed on his bike and pedalled away down the drive.

"Who was that?" Natalie asked.

"Ted Rogers, the new stablehand. He started last week – just turned up one day looking for work, which pleased Mum because we're really busy at the moment."

"So you don't know much about him?" Andi said, immediately suspicious.

"Not much, I suppose. But he's really good with horses."

Andi and Natalie exchanged glances. "Did he have references from his previous jobs?" Andi asked.

"I don't think so. Why?"

"Well, don't you think it's a bit of a coincidence that just after a new stablehand turns up, one of the ponies goes missing?"

Neil stared at her. "You don't mean . . .?"

"That Ted stole Sunshine? He might have done. Did he seem particularly interested in her?" Andi felt shaky inside: they could be really close to catching the thief!

"He likes all the horses. I haven't noticed that he has any special favourites." Neil ran a hand through his hair distractedly. "But lots of stuff's disappeared since Ted's been working here. I thought he was just putting things back in the wrong places, but there's no reason for him to have moved Badger's rug . . ." He tailed off.

"So maybe he's stolen it," Andi finished for him. "And maybe he's stolen Sunshine, too. If he's that good with horses, he'd have been able to make her go with him, even if she was a bit nervous." Her hopes were soaring. Perhaps this wasn't going to be such a hard case to solve, after all. "Come on, let's follow him!"

Chapter Eight

"Hang on, Andi," Natalie said. "It can't have been Ted who stole Sunshine. The police will have checked him out already, along with all the other staff at the centre."

"Maybe. But perhaps he hid Sunshine too well. You have to admit he looks suspicious."

"Well, I suppose . . ."

"OK, then!" Andi raced after Ted, desperate to keep him in sight, though he was pedalling fast. "We can't let him get away," she called over her shoulder.

"OK, OK." Natalie ran after her. "But there's no way we'll be able to keep up with him. I know you're a fast runner, Andi, but he's on his bike. You'll never catch him. And if *you* can't do it, *I* won't stand a chance."

"Take my bike. And my mum's," Neil said. "They're over here."

The bikes were distant relations of the mountain bikes they were more used to riding, but Andi wasn't going to let that stop her. "Quick, Nat!" She jumped on to the nearest bike and set off down the drive. "Look after Buddy for me, Neil!" she yelled over her shoulder.

"OK," Neil shouted back.

"Wait for me!" Natalie called.

Andi had to work hard on Neil's bike to keep up with Ted. Her legs pumped furiously as she bounced and rattled along the pot-holed drive, but she seemed to be making painfully slow progress. She tried clicking through the gears, but none of them made much difference to her speed. By the time she reached the road, Ted was a long way ahead and Andi's legs felt ready to drop off. But there was no way she was giving up now. This was their best lead yet!

Natalie drew level with her, red-faced and breathless. "I can't believe we're doing this!" she gasped.

"Just keep pedalling," Andi panted.

To her relief, the road began to slope downhill. She sat up straighter in the saddle and allowed the bike to freewheel. Ahead, she could see a pair of houses standing on a bend in the road. "I hope he lives in one of those houses," she said. "I don't want to ride much further on this boneshaker."

Sure enough, Ted skidded to a halt in front of the first house and went inside, leaving his bike propped against the porch.

"Thank goodness," Natalie groaned.

"Let's pull in here," Andi said when she and Natalie were about twenty metres from the house. An ivy-covered hedge grew alongside the road, and they pushed the bikes into it to hide them.

"What do we do now?" Natalie hunched over with her hands on her knees, trying to get her breath back.

"Let's look round. Perhaps Sunshine's round the back."

They walked down the hill with their hands in their pockets, trying to look like hikers out for an afternoon stroll. Andi scanned the windows as they approached the house, but nobody was looking out.

Ted's back garden was enclosed by a wood panel

fence about a metre high. They ducked down when they reached it, then crept along beside it. A gate led into the back garden. Natalie opened it cautiously, and they tiptoed through into a tangle of weeds and overgrown shrubs.

"He's not too keen on gardening, by the look of it," Andi breathed. Then she clutched Natalie's arm. A flat-roofed outbuilding stood at the bottom of the garden. It was the perfect place to keep a stolen pony!

"Are you sure this is a good idea?" Natalie whispered. "I mean, won't the police have already checked this place?"

"But what if they haven't?" Andi pointed out. "They might have been concentrating on finding the horsebox Shona saw, and not come here at all." She crept forward. "Sunshine could be just a few metres away, Nat."

"OK," Natalie said. "I suppose it would be daft not to check everywhere now we're here."

They tiptoed towards the shed, trying not to get snagged on the bushes. At the very bottom of the garden, the shrubs had been cleared, leaving a patch of bare mud.

"Yuck!" Natalie said in a low voice.

Slipping and sliding, they picked their way across the mud to the outbuilding. The door was bolted on the outside. "Why would anyone need to lock their shed right out here?" Andi whispered. "Suspicious or what!"

Natalie pressed her ear to the door. "I think you're right, Andi!" she gasped. "There is something in there. I can hear it moving about." Her eyes shone with excitement.

Andi listened too. Something big was bumping about inside.

"I suppose it might be Ted's own horse," Natalie whispered.

"I shouldn't think he's got one," Andi said. "Not if he rides a bike to the stables. No one would choose to cycle up that hill if they could let a horse carry them instead. He could easily leave it in the stable or the paddock all day." She grinned at Natalie. "Looks like the Pet Finders have done it again!"

"Let's get her out." Natalie seized the bolt and slid it back. As she pushed the door open, they heard a loud squeal. A moment later, an enormous bristly pig came charging out. It was pink and black, with beady eyes and sharp teeth. Natalie screamed and dived out of the way. She slipped in the mud and fell over, arms flailing.

The pig swerved and cannoned into Andi's legs. She stumbled back, her arms flapping wildly as she tried in vain to keep her balance. "Look out, Nat!" she screeched, as the pig came galloping back, snorting. She struggled to stand up but the mud was too slippery. Even getting on to her knees was difficult; all she could do was slither aside every time the pig charged.

Natalie lurched towards her, somehow managing to stay on her feet. She was plastered with mud from head to toe. She held out a filthy hand to Andi. "Let's get out of here."

"What's going on?" bellowed a furious voice.

Andi slithered round and felt her heart plummet into her very muddy trainers. Ted was standing at the edge of the muddy space, arms folded, glowering at them. Behind him was an elderly man, wearing slippers and smoking a pipe. He was grinning broadly.

Andi took Natalie's mud-caked hand and struggled to her feet. She looked round warily for the pig. It had stopped charging about and was

rubbing its back against the fence on the far side of the pen.

"Well?" Ted demanded, taking a step forward.

Andi couldn't think of a thing to say. They could hardly tell him the truth, that they'd suspected him of stealing Sunshine. She gazed at him blankly, shivering underneath her liberal coating of cold wet mud.

"I'm sorry," Natalie said. She turned an agonized gaze on Andi, struggling for an explanation. "We're – um, searching for a lost cat. We thought it might have hidden in your shed. We didn't realize there was a pig inside." She tried to flip her hair back from her face, but it was caked in mud and it just stuck to her hand.

"Is that so?" Ted said, clearly not believing a word.

"Looks like they wanted our Bessie," the older man said. "I reckon we should call the police."

Andi gulped. She could just imagine what her mum would say if she had to collect them from the police station.

"We weren't trying to steal your pig, honestly." Keeping a close eye on the pig, Natalie edged unsteadily towards the shed. She picked up what looked to Andi like a huge lump of mud.

The muddy lump turned out to be Natalie's rucksack. She brushed mud from the fastener, then unbuckled it. With a shaky hand, she took out a flyer for the Pet Finders Club and handed it to Ted. "See? That's us. The Pet Finders Club."

Ted scanned the flyer briefly, then passed it to his father.

"We're looking for a . . . a Russian blue cat," Andi said, remembering a valuable pedigree that they'd tracked down once.

"We've been searching everywhere," Natalie added.

The old man chewed the end of his pipe. "Maybe they're not thieves after all."

"Just what I was thinking," Ted agreed. "Though they could be pretty much anything under all that mud."

"So can we go then?" Andi asked, relieved that Ted didn't recognize them from the stables.

"I suppose so. But I wouldn't recommend coming back here. Our Bessie doesn't like being disturbed." Ted stepped aside so they could pass him.

All Andi wanted to do was run out of the garden, jump on Neil's bike and pedal away as fast as she could, but she and Natalie were ankle-deep in sticky mud. They squelched through it, hot with embarrassment, watched by the beady-eyed pig.

At last they were back on the road. They sped up past the cottage, though their mud-plastered trainers made their feet heavy and clumsy.

They retrieved their bikes from the hedge. "Thanks for that, Andi. Not!" Natalie said. "You almost got us arrested!"

Andi began to scrape mud off her trainers with a stick. "I know. Sorry. But it did look suspicious and—" She broke off.

Natalie was grinning at her, her teeth gleaming white in her filthy face. "You look like the Creature from the Slime Pit," she laughed.

"So do you."

Suddenly they both collapsed in helpless giggles. "We must have looked really stupid trying to run away from that pig!" Natalie hooted.

"Ted and his dad must have wondered what on earth we were up to!" Andi couldn't stop laughing. Then she remembered why they'd come here in the first place, and her high spirits drained away. "But we still haven't found Sunshine."

Natalie stopped giggling. "I know. We'd better get back to the stables."

They scraped off as much mud as they could, then rubbed their hands on the grass to clean them.

"I've got a bad feeling about this case," Andi admitted.

Natalie sighed. "Me too. I thought if we could find small animals like cats and dogs, then finding an animal as big as a pony would be a doddle. But it isn't." She ran her fingers through her mud-matted hair.

"The trouble is," Andi said, "if cats and dogs wander off, you can be pretty sure they haven't gone far from home. But if Sunshine's been stolen, then she could have been taken anywhere, even all the way to Scotland or right down south." She hated to admit it, but this was starting to look like one case they just weren't going to solve.

Next day, Andi took Buddy for a walk in the park after school. She'd arranged to meet Natalie and Tristan there, and they were waiting by the entrance. Natalie had brought Jet, her black Labrador, with her.

"Hi, Andi," Tristan said. "I see you've managed to clean off all the mud."

"So, you've heard about our great pig adventure."

Tristan grinned. "Natalie told me. Wish I'd been there to see it for myself. You could at least have taken some photos."

They went into the park and Andi let Buddy off his lead. He went haring away, then circled back, as though he were a sheepdog and they were a flock of sheep. Jet watched him wistfully. "It's no good you looking like that, Jet," Natalie said. He had a habit of running off when he was let off his lead.

"Why don't you take him to dog school?" Andi suggested. "Labradors are usually easy to train."

"Yeah, that's not a bad idea," said Natalie thoughtfully.

"Did you find any more clues?" Tristan asked as they headed towards the woods.

"Neil said that some things have gone missing at the stables," Andi told him. "Badger's rug for a start. And there's a new stablehand—"

"Oh, didn't I tell you?" Natalie cut in. "Neil

phoned me today. He asked Ted about the missing things, but he doesn't know anything about them. Neil's certain he hasn't taken them."

"Well at least that means we won't have to meet up with his pig again," Andi said.

"Whoa!" Tristan yelled suddenly. He darted away.

"Tristan?" Andi called after him. "Has he just seen someone delivering fresh-baked cakes or something?" she joked to Natalie.

"No, look!" Natalie grabbed her arm. "It's that horsebox. It totally fits the description of the horsebox Shona saw driving too fast on the day Sunshine was stolen!"

Andi looked where she was pointing. Sure enough, a green horsebox with a smashed-in wing was driving along the road next to the park!

Chapter Nine

The lorry turned left. Tristan came haring back to them. "Quick! That road leads round the back of the woods. He'll come out in Half Mile Lane. We can cut across the middle of the park and head him off." He pelted in the opposite direction.

"Oh no, not more running!" Natalie groaned. All the same, she raced after Tristan, with Jet loping beside her.

Andi whistled for Buddy. He was quite a distance away, down by the lake, but he came scampering over, barking with excitement. "Come on, Bud." Andi sprinted after Natalie and Tristan. Buddy kept pace easily with her, his mouth open in a wide doggy grin: there was nothing he liked better than a good run.

Normally, Andi could outrun Tristan and Natalie easily. Today, to her surprise, it took her a couple of minutes to catch up with either of them. She passed Natalie first. She was red-faced and panting hard, but she showed no signs of giving up. Tristan was a little way ahead, running strongly.

Wow! Andi thought. *Being in the Pet Finders Club must be getting them into shape!*

Pushing herself harder, she caught up with Tristan, then raced on to the gate. She stooped down and clipped on Buddy's lead before heading out to the pavement. "Come on, boy. Let's see if we can find that horsebox." There was no sign of it yet: it must still be driving along the winding road that ran through the trees to the west of the park.

Tristan pounded up to join her. Panting hard, he looked hopefully along the road in both directions. A few moments later, Natalie arrived with Jet. "Can – you – see – it?" she gasped.

"Not yet," Andi admitted.

Natalie clung to the park railings, trying to get her breath back.

Suddenly the green horsebox appeared at the

top of the hill. "There it is!" Andi exclaimed.

Sensing her excitement, Buddy began to bark.

"Er, what are we going to do now?" Tristan asked, looking uncertain.

"We can't just let it drive past," Natalie protested. "This is our best chance of cracking this case."

"What do you suggest? That we all jump out into the road to stop it and then accuse the driver of being a horse thief?" Tristan said scornfully.

"Hang on," Andi said. "It's turning." The lorry was slowing down next to a junction. "Where does that road go, Tris?"

His face lit up. "The lorry drivers' rest stop! Don't you remember, we went there looking for Apple's owner?" They'd found Apple, a cute terrier, in a back garden not far from Andi's house.

"Let's go. Come on, Jet." Natalie began to jog along the road.

Andi and Tristan sped after her.

They soon reached the drivers' rest stop. "Can you see the horsebox?" Tristan asked.

"There!" Natalie shrieked. The green horsebox was parked between two enormous juggernauts, its dent with the red scrape of paint clearly visible. The driver was still inside, rummaging through the glove compartment. As they approached, he snapped it shut and climbed out. He was a stocky man with bushy grey hair.

Andi stepped back hurriedly as the man looked round, and her foot came down on top of Tristan's. The horsebox driver walked towards the café, whistling.

"Let's check the horsebox," Tristan whispered, standing on one leg and rubbing his toes. "Perhaps Sunshine's hidden in the back."

Andi's knees were quaking as they crept to the horsebox. She pressed her ear to the door. There was no sound, but perhaps Sunshine was standing still – or lying down, hurt!

Checking that nobody was watching them, they stole along the side of the horsebox to the groom's door just behind the cab. Tristan seized the handle. To Andi's surprise, it wasn't locked. The rusty hinges grated as they tried to open it, making them all freeze: surely somebody must have heard! But nobody came running to demand what they were doing.

They swung the door open and boosted Andi up so she could see inside. The floor of the horsebox was strewn with straw and an empty haynet hung from a ring on the side, but there was no sign of Sunshine.

"She's not here," Andi said, disappointed.

"He must have taken her somewhere else," Natalie groaned. "He's got to be the thief. Why else would he have been belting away from the stables on the very day that Sunshine vanished?"

"What do we do now?" Tristan asked.

"I'm going to talk to the driver." Natalie thrust Jet's lead into Tristan's hand and strode away, heading in the direction of the café.

Andi and Tristan ran after her. "Wait!" Andi caught her arm. "What are you going to say?"

Natalie was grim-faced. "I'll think of something."

The driver was still chatting outside the café.

"Excuse me," Natalie said, stepping forward. "I couldn't help noticing the horse stickers on the windscreen of your lorry. Do you know the way to Riverside Stables?"

The driver looked round. "I most certainly do. I must have driven past it at least a dozen times last week. I was trying to find a farm in the mountains and I had to keep turning round. I thought I'd never get there!"

Natalie glanced over her shoulder at Andi and Tristan, before going on. "I hear they've got some gorgeous horses there. At Riverside, I mean."

The second driver, a plump man in his early fifties, grinned. "It sounds right up your street, Mac."

"Oh, do you like horses then?" Natalie asked. Andi was amazed at the way she made the question sound so casual. She was glad she hadn't had to speak to the driver herself; she probably wouldn't have been able to think of a thing to say.

"Can't stand them," Mac said unexpectedly. "Scared stiff, to tell the truth. I was kicked by a New Forest pony when I was young – broke my arm, it did. I've never been near a horse since."

"But your lorry—" Natalie began.

"Oh, yes. Well, I bought it from a showjumper a few months ago, but I just use it for transporting cattle. They're a lot easier to handle, I can tell you! Now about those directions to Riverside

Stables . . ." He glanced round and his eye lighted on Andi. "Are you three together?"

"I – um . . ." Natalie gasped.

Too late, Andi realized that she was wearing a Riverside Stables T-shirt. The logo was showing and the horsebox driver must have noticed it. She pulled her coat across, but the damage was done.

"Look, I don't know what game you're playing," he snapped, "but if your friend's got a Riverside Stables shirt then she obviously knows the way already." He stalked into the café.

Natalie scooted back to Andi and Tristan. "He can't be the thief if he's scared of horses."

"I suppose not," Andi agreed. "He'd never be able to get Sunshine into his horsebox."

"Perhaps he was lying," Tristan pointed out. "I mean, he might have told people he was scared of horses so no one would suspect him when horses started disappearing."

"But what are we going to do?" Andi said. "We can't follow him when he leaves here. He's in a lorry. We won't be able to keep up."

"And he's pretty scary," Natalie said. "Did you see the way he looked when he spotted Andi's T-shirt?

I'm not sure I'd want to go snooping round his farm looking for Sunshine."

"He's our best lead," Tristan said determinedly. "And I'm not giving up with him just yet. Let's hide near his horsebox and see what he does when he comes out. Or . . ." His eyes gleamed. "We could hide in the back and find out where he goes."

"No!" Andi exclaimed. "That would be way too dangerous!"

"OK, OK, it was just an idea! But there's no harm in watching what he does."

They headed back towards the horsebox and hid behind a huge juggernaut nearby. "Wait here and keep watch," Tristan said.

"Why? What are you going to do?" Natalie asked.

"I'm going to see if his cab's unlocked." Tristan checked all round then darted to the horsebox.

"Tristan!" Andi called after him. "Come back!"

He tried the door and it swung open.

"It's open," Natalie groaned. "Come on. We'd better go and see what he's up to."

She and Andi ran to the lorry. Tristan was already inside, peering into the glove compartment.

He pulled out a tattered pamphlet and leafed through it. "He was telling the truth," he sighed. "He *does* use his lorry for cattle. Look at this." The pamphlet was a programme from a cattle sale. "He's ringed some of the cows in here, so he must have been a genuine customer." Sighing, Tristan thrust the programme back in the glove compartment. "It looks like his story's starting to add up."

He jumped down from the cab and shut the door.

"Quick!" Natalie gasped. "The driver's coming back."

They dashed behind the next lorry and waited, hearts thumping, until they heard the horsebox drive away.

"This is hopeless!" Andi groaned as they trudged back across the park. "That horsebox was our only lead, but the driver obviously isn't the thief."

"We've hardly made a start on this case at all," Tristan said gloomily. "And—" He was interrupted by Natalie's phone ringing.

She pulled it out of her bag and checked the caller ID. "Hmm, I don't recognize this number."

"Perhaps it's a new case," Andi said, perking up.

"Preferably an easy one," Tristan added. "Like a cat stuck up a tree, surrounded by people pointing at it."

Natalie answered the phone, switching it to speakerphone so they could all hear. "You're looking for a missing pony," said a gruff voice.

"Who is this?" Natalie gasped.

"That doesn't matter. The pony's fine, okay? She doesn't need to be found." The line went dead.

"That was the thief!" Andi exclaimed. "We just spoke to the thief!"

"And by the sound of it they were disguising their voice," Tristan said. "Nobody really speaks like that. You couldn't even tell if it was a man or woman."

Natalie grabbed a pen and a notepad from her bag and jotted down the caller's number. "Weird number! It ends in four eights."

"Try ringing back," Andi said eagerly. Then she shivered. "Though I'm not sure I want to speak to them again. They sounded really creepy. Perhaps we should just call the police."

"We can't let a lead like this one go." Natalie punched the redial button. The thief's phone began to ring.

Andi held her breath, waiting for someone to answer, though she couldn't imagine what they'd say. Natalie hung on for ages, but the phone just rang and rang. In the end, they were cut off automatically. "Why did the thief say the pony doesn't need to be found?" she wondered. "And how did they know we were looking for Sunshine?"

"They must have seen one of the flyers Nat left and guessed that we'd be involved," Tristan said. "But that was a weird thing to say, that Sunshine doesn't *need* to be found. Of course she does. Her owner wants her back. Even a really stupid thief would know that."

"He was just trying to scare us off," Natalie decided. "But he obviously doesn't know the Pet Finders very well. One anonymous phone call isn't going to stop us!"

They headed to Tristan's house to talk about what to do next. Mrs Saunders beamed at them as they came into the kitchen. "Good timing! I've just made some flapjacks."

They followed her into the kitchen, a homely

room with a big square table at one end. "Sit down. Juice and flapjacks all round?"

"You bet!" Tristan whooped.

Mrs Saunders frowned when they told her about the phone call. "This is getting a bit serious for my liking."

"They didn't threaten us or anything, Mrs Saunders," Natalie said. She broke off a piece of flapjack and dropped it on the floor for Jet. He stood up, his tail wagging, but Buddy was too quick for him and snatched the piece of flapjack before he could eat it. Jet flopped down again good-naturedly.

Buddy leapt up at Natalie, clearly hoping for another piece of flapjack. He knocked her hand and her phone went flying.

"Bad Buddy," Andi scolded. "No more flapjack for you."

She bent down to pick up the phone, then froze. The redial button must have been pressed as it hit the floor because Andi could hear a voice coming from the phone.

"Yes? Yes? Is anyone there?" a man said impatiently.

"What was the last number you rang, Nat?" Andi hissed.

Natalie gasped. "It was the thief's number. The one ending in four eights!"

Chapter Ten

"H-hello," Andi said into the phone, hardly able to believe that she was talking to a horse thief.

"Hello there. Can I help?" the man said. He sounded brisk but quite friendly – not at all like the gruff scary voice that had called before.

"I – I'm calling about the missing horse," Andi faltered.

"A missing horse? Why are you ringing a café about a missing horse?"

"What? You're in a *café*?"

"Young lady, I am always in this café. I own this café, and I spend eighteen hours a day here."

"Oh." Andi thought for a moment. "So this is a payphone I'm ringing?"

"That's right."

"Someone rang us from this phone about half an hour ago. Do you know who it was?"

"I'm sorry, I really haven't got time for this right now. I've got a whole load of customers waiting to be served. Hang on a minute, Emma. That man wanted a side salad! Look, I've got to go."

"Wait! Don't hang up! What's the name of your café?"

"The Bird's Nest." The line went dead.

Andi told Natalie and Tristan what the café owner had said. "It's called The Bird's Nest," she finished.

"The Bird's Nest Café?" Mrs Saunders echoed. "I know where that is. We sold a farmhouse just along the road from there." She fetched a map and spread it out on the table. "It's on this road here."

"That's not far from Riverside Stables!" Tristan looked hopefully at his mum. "Um . . . how do you feel about getting out of the house, Mum? I mean, you've been cooped up inside making flapjacks and—"

"Tristan, I am *not* driving you to meet a horse thief! Let's call the police and let them handle it."

"But, Mrs Saunders, the thief won't still be at the café," Natalie said.

"And we can't call the police unless we've got something definite to tell them," Andi added persuasively. "If we go to the café we can get a description of the man who used the phone."

"Come on, Mum," Tristan begged.

Mrs Saunders sighed. "All right, I suppose. But I'm coming in with you. And if the thief's still there, we're coming straight out again. Is that clear?"

"Yes. Thanks, Mum." Tristan drained the last of his juice. "Come on!"

The Bird's Nest Café was set on a narrow side road about three miles from Riverside Stables. It was a square single-storey building with a life-sized plastic robin outside. The name was painted in red letters above the door.

They left Buddy and Jet in the car and hurried inside. "Wow, this place is really *themed*," Natalie whispered in Andi's ear.

The waitresses were wearing brown baseball caps with birds' wings, heads and tails attached. Enormous photos of birds hung on the walls and bird models dangled from the ceiling, turning in slow circles. A menu was chalked on a blackboard behind the counter. "Mmm, that buzzard burger with grilled aubergine sounds nice," Tristan said.

"We haven't come here to eat," Natalie reminded him sternly.

"I'll be here," Mrs Saunders said, taking a table near the door where she'd have a good view of the whole café. "Perhaps I'll have a coffee while you're asking questions."

A door led into the kitchen. It stood open and they could see a man in a striped apron chopping onions. "Hot dog's almost ready," he called.

"That's the man I spoke to on the phone," Andi said, recognizing his voice. She darted to the counter and waved to attract his attention. To her annoyance, he turned away without noticing.

"I won't keep you a minute," said the woman behind the counter. She set down a mug of coffee in front of one of the customers. "There you go, Tom." She turned to the Pet Finders. "Hello there. What can I get you?"

"We're trying to find someone who made a call from the payphone here an hour or so ago," Andi said.

"Sorry, I only started work twenty minutes

ago. But Emma's been here all morning." She raised her voice across the café: "Emma, people to see you!"

Emma, a young waitress with long red hair tied in a ponytail, came hurrying over, tucking her order pad into the wide pocket on the front of her denim skirt. She looked at them curiously.

"We're trying to find a stolen pony," Tristan explained. "Someone rang us about her from your payphone about an hour ago."

Frowning, Emma pushed back her hat, setting the wings wobbling. "Well, a few people have used the phone today. A couple of men in a pick-up truck. And a man with a puncture who phoned the garage to come and fix it."

"Did you know any of them?" Andi asked eagerly.

"No. Just passing, I suppose, and called in for a coffee."

"What did they look like, these men who made the calls?" Natalie prompted.

Emma frowned. "The pick-up truck men were in their mid-twenties, I'd say. And wearing denim jackets. The other chap had a beard and was a bit overweight."

"Did you hear what they said?" Tristan questioned.

"No chance!" Emma nodded towards the kitchen. "If Mr Crowe thought I was standing round listening to phone conversations, he'd have something to say."

"So it could have been any one of those three men who called us," Tristan said thoughtfully. They started to head for the door.

"Oh, wait," Emma said, calling them back. "There was a girl, too."

"Did she use the phone?" Andi asked.

"Yes, she did. But she only made a very short call. I asked her if she needed any help – she looked a bit upset – but she left in a hurry."

"Can you remember what she looked like?" said Tristan.

"Quite tall and very thin. She had fair hair, cropped short."

Andi gasped. That sounded exactly like Sara, the girl who had gone missing! Could it have been her who made the call to Natalie? Did that mean *she'd* stolen Sunshine?

The man who'd been chopping onions appeared

at the kitchen door. "Emma, I don't pay you to stand round talking all day!"

Emma jumped. "I've got to get going," she said. "I hope you find the pony." She began to clear one of the tables.

"But there are other questions we need to ask you," Natalie said.

"No, it's OK," Andi told her. "I know who it is!" She dragged Natalie and Tristan outside. She could hardly believe it. How could Sara be the thief?

"What on earth are you talking about?" Natalie pulled herself free and smoothed down her jacket.

"I recognized the description Emma gave us." Andi sank down on the low wall surrounding the café. "It's Sara! You know, the girl who ran away." Shakily, she told them about Sara's weird behaviour at the riding centre. "She kept looking at Sunshine all the time. And she wanted to ride her, but Shona wouldn't let her."

Tristan sat beside her. "She wouldn't have taken Sunshine just because of that." He broke off as a man came out of the café and climbed into a car, then continued: "There has to be some other reason."

Andi shrugged. "She probably wasn't thinking straight. Perhaps she really wanted a pony of her own, but her parents wouldn't let her have one. Right now, it doesn't matter why she did it, but we've got to find her before the police do. She's in real trouble and perhaps we can help." She jumped up and gazed round, but there was no way of knowing which direction Sara had taken when she left the café.

"It'd be better if she brought Sunshine back herself," Natalie said, "rather than wait until she's hunted down by the police."

"So we'd better start searching," Tristan said. "She can't be far from here because she was in this café only an hour ago." He broke off and his anxious look faded. "Didn't you say her aunt lived on a farm?"

"Halfpenny Farm. It's not far from Andi's house," Natalie told him. "And it's not all that far from here either, if you're on horseback and can cut across country."

"I bet she's there!" Tristan exclaimed. "There are probably loads of outbuildings where she could hide. And she'd guess her aunt has gone to help her mum look for her closer to home."

Mrs Saunders came out of the café. "You were quick. I hardly had time to finish my coffee. Did you find out anything?"

"Loads. We'll tell you in the car," Tristan said. "Right now we need to get back to Aldcliffe quick!"

They scrambled into the car. Buddy leapt on to Andi's lap the moment she sat down, and began to lick her furiously.

Tristan told his mum what they'd found out. "You should ring the police," she said. "This is important. The sooner that poor girl is back home the better."

"I'll do it," Natalie said.

"Right, let's go." Mrs Saunders started the engine. She paused with her hands on the steering wheel and met Andi's eyes in the mirror. "Oh that poor girl," she said, echoing Andi's thoughts. "I do hope you find her soon."

Natalie pulled out her mobile as the car sped away. "Oh no! The battery's flat."

"Never mind. We'll ring from Halfpenny Farm," Andi said. "And hopefully we'll be able to tell the police that we've solved two cases in one."

* * *

144

Sara's uncle, Mr Walker, came sprinting down the drive when Mrs Saunders' car pulled up. "Oh," he said flatly as the Pet Finders scrambled out. "Can I help you? I thought you might be bringing news of my niece."

"We are!" Andi exclaimed. "We think we know where she might be. She's taken a pony from Riverside Stables and we think she's hiding in one of your outbuildings."

Mr Walker stared at her. "Taken a pony? Hiding here?"

"We think she called us from a café near the stables just over an hour ago, so she must be hiding somewhere not too far away. This seems like a pretty good place to start looking."

"Come on, then." Mr Walker led the way to the first barn and threw open the door. The Pet Finders crowded inside, squinting into the gloom. There were a couple of pieces of farm machinery in the shadows, but that was all.

"No sign of her in here," Andi said, disappointed.

They ran to the next barn, and the next, but Sara and Sunshine were nowhere to be found. "I really thought we were on to something," Tristan sighed.

"Is there anywhere else on the farm where she could hide?"

"Not really." Mr Walker frowned. "Where on earth can she be? And why would she steal a pony? I know she was upset when Buttercup was stolen, but that was a year ago. It can't be anything to do with that."

"Can we use your phone, please, Mr Walker?" Natalie asked. "We ought to tell the police what we've found out."

Andi's heart sank. She knew the police had to be told what was going on, but she'd really hoped the Pet Finders would find Sara first.

"Yes, of course." Mr Walker led the way to the farmhouse. Buddy pressed close against Andi's leg, as though he could sense her disappointment and wanted to cheer her up.

"I don't suppose you've got a photo of Sara that we could borrow, have you, Mr Walker?" Andi asked as they went inside. "We could show it to the waitress at the café, just to make sure that it really was Sara who made the call."

"Here you are." Mr Walker took a photo from the living-room mantelpiece and handed it to her.

Sara was beaming into the camera beside a well-groomed buckskin pony who wore a big red rosette on her bridle.

Andi glanced at it, then gasped in astonishment. "This is Sunshine!"

"No, that's Buttercup," Mr Walker corrected. "Sara's pony that was stolen last summer."

Andi looked at the photo more closely. "This pony hasn't got a freeze brand, but it is *definitely* Sunshine. Look, you can see the dark stripe in her tail."

Tristan, Natalie and Mr Walker stared at her, horror-struck. "So Sunshine was really Sara's stolen pony, Buttercup?" Tristan said. "No wonder Sara kept staring while you were riding her, Andi. She must have been amazed to find her after all this time!"

"But how did she end up at the O'Connors' riding school?" Andi wondered. "You don't think . . .?" She trailed off, hardly able to believe the suspicion that was forming in her mind.

"That the O'Connors are horse thieves?" Tristan finished for her in a shocked voice.

Andi shivered. "They can't be," she whispered. But what other explanation was there?

"What did the police say, Nat?" Andi asked, as the Pet Finders headed back to Andi's house. Natalie had made the call while she and Tristan were looking at Sara's photo. They had left Mr Walker trying to get in touch with Sara's parents to tell them the latest news, which was both more hopeful and more startling than anything else so far.

"They're sending someone to the café to talk to Emma." Natalie sighed. "And I expect they'll want to interview the O'Connors, too."

Andi squeezed her arm. Poor Nat! It had been a shock for all of them to discover that the O'Connors had probably stolen Sunshine, but it was worse for her because she was so fond of Neil. "Mrs O'Connor seemed so nice," she said. "I wonder if any of their other horses are stolen."

"Perhaps we're wrong about all this," Tristan suggested, as they turned into Andi's road. "Perhaps there are two buckskin ponies with dark stripes in their tail."

"I doubt it," Andi said. It would be a pretty unlikely coincidence for Sara to be involved with two ponies with the same unusual colouring.

"When we get to your house, I'm going to call Neil and ask him where they got Sunshine," Natalie decided.

"Don't tell him about the photo," Andi warned. "We don't want the O'Connors realizing we're on to them and hiding any evidence."

"It's probably too late to worry about that," Tristan pointed out. "I expect the police are there now, questioning them."

Andi's mum was upstairs in her study when they went in. "Hello!" she called.

"Hello, Mum. Is it OK to make a phone call?"

"Of course, darling."

The Pet Finders huddled round the phone. Natalie's hands were shaking as she dialled the number of the riding stables. Andi squeezed her arm, wishing she could make her feel better.

There was a tense pause while they waited for someone to answer the phone.

"Hello, Riverside Stables." It was Neil's voice.

"Hello, Neil. This is Natalie." Her voice was squeaky with strain.

"Is there any news? Have you found Sunshine?" He sounded genuinely concerned, but Andi was sure he was acting so they wouldn't suspect anything.

"No, not yet. Listen, we were wondering . . ." Natalie frowned while she worked out what to say. "We were wondering where you got Sunshine. I mean, if she got loose, she might have tried to head back to where she came from."

"Oh, right." He paused. "Hang on, I'm trying to remember."

Andi pulled a face at Tristan. Neil could be frantically trying to work out a believable story.

"I'm fairly sure we bought her from a dealer in Yorkshire," he continued. "It would be a long way for her to go and she'd have to cross quite a few main roads to get back there, so I hope she hasn't tried it. But it's a good idea. I'll give them a ring to see if she's turned up."

Natalie gave Andi and Tristan a thumbs-up. "Good idea. Let us know how you get on." She hung up, beaming. "See, I knew Neil wasn't a thief!"

"But what he said doesn't prove anything," Tristan pointed out. "He didn't give us the name of the dealer, did he? He might just be a good liar, Nat."

"No, he's not! You're wrong about him!" Natalie

glowered at Tristan. "You don't even know him!"

Andi stepped between them. "Look, arguing isn't going to help find Sara and Sunshine. We need to get back to the stables. There's still a chance we could find her before the police do, and let her know that everyone's only trying to help. We know she's not too far from the café, which means they're probably hiding out in the mountains." She glanced out of the window and shivered. Heavy black clouds were building up. "We'll have to hurry. It looks like there's storm coming. And it'll be dark soon, too."

Mrs Talbot came running downstairs. "Is there any news?"

Andi told her about their startling discovery, that the runaway girl, Sara, might have tried to steal back her own pony. "We're going out to the stables again. We think Sara and Sunshine are hiding in the mountains."

"We'd better get a move on," Natalie said. "The bus to Riverside Stables leaves in ten minutes."

Tristan glanced at his watch and groaned. "I didn't realize it was so late. I'm meant to be at Paws for Thought in twenty minutes. A rep's coming in to talk to Christine about snakes, and I don't want to miss him. You'll have to go without me, but phone me if you find anything." He darted out of the front door.

"I'm not sure that you should go back to the stables today," Mrs Talbot said. "I don't like the look of that sky and it's getting late. Leave it to the police to find Sara."

"Oh, Mum, we've *got* to go. Sara must be so frightened out there all on her own."

"And she might stay hidden if she sees the police," Natalie added. "Perhaps she'll come out for us."

Andi could see that her mum was wavering. "Please, Mum," she begged. "We're really worried about her."

"OK then. I'll give you a lift. But promise me you won't do anything silly, Andi."

"I promise." Andi grabbed her coat and sped out of the house.

Chapter Eleven

By the time they reached Riverside Stables, the sky was as black as tar. The clouds were so low they looked as if they were resting on the mountain-tops, and the wind was raging.

As they leapt out of the car, Neil came racing across the yard with an armful of halters. Andi blinked. It was so hard to imagine that he was a horse thief!

"Can you give me a hand?" He had to shout to make himself heard above the screech of the wind. "I need to get the horses in." He didn't seem to be acting as though he had anything to hide. Perhaps Natalie was right, and he had been telling the truth about the dealer after all.

Andi and Natalie followed him, battling against

the ferocious wind every step of the way. The surface of the duck pond had been chopped into waves that splashed against the bank. Andi spotted the ducks sheltering under bushes, heads down and tails turned to the wind.

The red-and-white cows stood in a huddle in their open-fronted shelter at the far end of the field. "Should we bring the cows in too?" Natalie yelled.

"No. Their coats will give them enough protection," Neil shouted back. "And their shelter faces away from the wind. They'll be fine."

The horses were clustered round the gate, stamping their hooves nervously. Neil slipped a halter over Scrumpy's head, and thrust the lead-rope into Andi's hand. "Do you think you can manage two?"

"Yeah."

Neil caught Chipper. The sorrel pony was jumpy, but Neil calmed him by stroking his nose and speaking to him in a low voice. He passed Andi the rope, then caught Tilly, Bonnie and Flash. Natalie took charge of Tilly while Neil led the others.

As they crossed the field, rain began to fall. By

the time they reached the stable, it was like standing under a tap. Andi's hair was so wet it was plastered to her head.

"The police have been," Neil said, as they settled the horses into the stables, which were warm and cosy and smelt deliciously of clean straw. "They told us Sunshine used to belong to Sara. Poor girl, I can't believe we bought a stolen pony." He hugged Flash. "I don't know what I'd do if somebody took Flash." He paused, then added, "You must have thought we were horse thieves!"

Andi gulped, but Natalie answered straight-faced. "No! Of course not!"

"We gave the dealer's details to the police," Neil continued, "so they'll know we bought her fair and square. And now I suppose you're planning to search for Sara and Sunshine on the mountain."

"That's right." Andi listened to the rain pounding on the roof and the wind screeching round the stable. "We'd better get going before the storm gets any worse."

"I'll come with you," Neil said. "And we'll take the horses. It'll be quicker that way. Andi, you ride Chipper, and Nat, you can take Bonnie. They'll be the calmest in this weather." He frowned. "I wish Mum could come too, but she's taken Donna to the farrier. She lost a shoe this morning."

While she saddled Chipper, Andi racked her brains, trying to work out where Sara might be hiding. She'd need shelter in weather like this. But there were hardly any buildings on the mountain. Suddenly an image popped into her head of some outbuildings clustered high on the mountainside. "Riverside Farm!" she burst out. "I bet Sara's taken Sunshine there! Shona pointed it out on our ride, so she knows about it."

Neil looked at her over the stable partition. He paused with his hands resting on Flash's saddle. "You could be right," he agreed. "We'll go up there first — as long as the road hasn't been washed away in the storm."

Andi gulped. Finding Sunshine was turning out to be even more of an adventure than they were used to!

Neil led the way through the woods with Natalie close behind him on Bonnie. Andi followed on Chipper. He was smaller than Sunshine, and not quite so co-operative: Andi had to urge him forward all the time to keep up with the others. The reins slipped in her wet hands and her sodden jeans clung uncomfortably to her legs. Rain dripped from the branches overhead, and the wind sang like a choir of ghosts and whipped rat-tails of wet hair into her face. Shivering violently, she pictured her cosy living room and wished she was back there, curled up on the sofa with Buddy.

"Come on," Neil called. "We need to cross the river before it gets too high."

Andi's heart lurched and she tried not to think about how they were going to get back again.

Flash broke into a trot, and Bonnie and Chipper sped up too. Chipper stopped at the edge of the trees and side-stepped restlessly. Andi patted his wet neck. "Sorry, boy, but we can't stop now." She tapped his sides with her heels and he started forward again.

The ground dropped into a dry gully immediately outside the wood, then climbed again more steeply than ever. Neil turned in his saddle and called back, "Let Chipper have his head. He'll be able to find the best path."

158

Andi slackened the reins and Chipper picked his way up the slope. Suddenly Flash stumbled on a loose stone. He lurched to one side, sending Neil toppling out of the saddle. He hit the ground hard.

"Neil!" Natalie screamed, leaping off Bonnie.

Andi jumped down from Chipper's back. Keeping a tight hold on his reins, she ran forward, her heart hammering. Neil was hunched on the ground. His face was very pale and he was biting his lip. Andi caught Flash's reins, then knelt beside him. "Are you all right?"

"I – I think so."

Natalie gripped Neil's arm. "Aagh! Let go!" he gasped, as she tried to help him up. "I think I've hurt my collarbone." He clutched his shoulder, looking whiter than ever.

"What are we going to do?" Natalie looked petrified. "You can't ride like this."

"Leave me here," Neil said. "You'll have to keep going. If the river floods, Sara could be trapped!"

Andi thought hard. They couldn't leave Neil out in the open, but they didn't have time to take him all the way back to the stables. Suddenly she remembered the boulder where the snake had frightened Sunshine. "The rock!" she cried, raising her voice as a gust of wind swept her words away. "You can shelter there!"

"Right." Catching Andi's hand, Neil hauled himself, slowly and painfully, to his feet. He rested for a moment, leaning on Flash and waiting for the pain to subside. "OK, let's go."

They settled Neil on the sheltered side of the boulder. He leant back and shut his eyes, his face creased with pain. "Take Flash for Sara to ride. Sunshine might not be up to carrying her if she's been living rough for a few days. Now get going. And good luck!" He tried to smile encouragingly at them, but his mouth was twisted with pain.

Andi and Natalie climbed on to the horses and set off again. Andi rode in front, leading Flash beside her and trying to remember where the shallow river crossing was. Night was coming and the light was fading fast now.

"Look!" Natalie shouted, pointing up the mountain.

Shielding her eyes, Andi peered into the rain. She could just make out the ruined buildings high above them. A light glimmered for a moment against one of the dark shapes and then went out. *It was probably just lightning reflecting off a window,* Andi told herself. *There's bound to be some thunder with rain as heavy as this. But it could have been the flash of a torch . . .*

Soon they could hear the river, though they couldn't see it in the gathering dark. Andi took a torch out of her saddlebag and shone it ahead. The thin yellow beam lit up the water rushing by, grey and swirling as it broke over jutting rocks.

"We'll never get across!" Natalie gasped.

"It's shallower further along."

They turned left and rode beside the river. At last it widened and the water flowed more slowly. Andi halted Chipper and shone the light down into the water. She could see the bottom quite clearly. "There! That's where we cross."

She urged Chipper forward until he was right at the water's edge, placing a hand on his neck to calm him. "I'll go across first." Andi handed Flash's reins to Natalie, then rode into the water. It swirled and splashed round Chipper's hooves, but the current wasn't strong enough to cause him any problems. In a few seconds Andi was on the far bank.

She turned and shone the torch out over the water. "It's OK, Nat."

Natalie rode into the beam of light, leading Flash. The water surged round the horses' legs but they kept going and scrambled out on to the bank.

They climbed the grassy slope, shoulders hunched against the rain. "How much further?" Natalie groaned. "We seem to have been going for ages."

At last they reached the steep, narrow track that led up to Riverside Farm. It was deeply rutted and covered in shards of loose rock. Rain was pouring down in dozens of little streams, carrying mud and pebbles down to the forest below.

Andi shone the torch up the mountainside; the beam was just strong enough to pick out the steep cliff with the farm buildings perched precariously on the edge. "We're almost there!"

They started up the road, but the horses' feet kept sliding on the loose stones. Chipper whinnied with fear. "It's OK, boy." Andi patted his neck. "You're doing fine."

The pony took another hesitant step and slid again. Andi looked over her shoulder. Bonnie was struggling, too. "Perhaps we should walk up this bit." She dismounted, then led Chipper uphill. Without her weight on his back, the pony was more surefooted and they were soon at the top.

Andi waited while Natalie brought Bonnie and Flash up the steep slope, then they made their way to the gate that led into the yard. It hung open on one hinge, its bottom rail resting on the ground.

"We made it," Andi said, gazing up at the old clapboard farmhouse. Rain streamed off the dilapidated roof and somewhere a barn door crashed in the wind. Suddenly the light flashed again, shining from the doorway of an old cattle shed. That wasn't lightning. There was someone here!

"Sara must be here!" Andi gasped. "Hold Chipper, Nat."

She ran across the muddy cobbled yard to the cowshed. She hesitated at the door: the shadows inside looked deep and frightening, and she remembered Shona saying the old farm looked haunted. *Those are just stories*, Andi told herself sternly. *If Sara's in there, she needs our help.* Mustering all her courage, she stepped inside, her feet crunching over broken tiles.

The cattle shed was divided into two stalls. Andi peered round the partitions, hardly daring to breathe. There was a tall, pale-looking figure in the second stall, huddled against the wooden partition with her knees pulled up to her chin. She was wrapped in a horse blanket, but she still looked frozen. Sunshine stood beside her, draped in another rug.

"Sara!"

Sara jumped up, startled. She looked terrified and ready to take off into the storm.

"Wait!" said Andi, holding out both hands. "It's me, Andi. We met on the trail ride, remember? I've come to fetch you. Everyone's really worried about you."

Tears welled up in Sara's eyes, but she brushed them away impatiently. "I'm not coming. I'm staying here."

"You can't. It's freezing."

"I don't care!"

Andi thought desperately. She had to persuade Sara to trust her – and fast, before the river got too deep for them to cross. "Look, I know Sunshine's really your pony, Buttercup."

Sara frowned. "How do you know? Nobody knows except me. I told my mum and dad I'd found her, but they didn't believe me," she said bitterly. "Do they think I wouldn't recognize my own pony?" She ran her fingers through Sunshine's mane. They were shaking violently, Andi noticed. "I had to get her back. I had to!"

Andi's head was whirling. Sara was clearly determined not to be parted from Sunshine again, but the O'Connors had bought her fairly from the dealer, just like Neil had said. Perhaps they'd get to keep her now, not Sara. It was such a mess! Andi shook her head. Whatever was going to happen, there was no way Sara could stay here. "You can't keep a pony in a place like this, Sara," she said. "I'm not a horse expert, but even I know they need proper stabling and care."

"We won't be here much longer." Sara ran her hands down the pony's shoulder, pulling the rug tighter across her chest. "Buttercup trod on a stone and went lame, but she'll be better in a couple of days. I'm going to take her home and prove to my parents that she really *is* Buttercup. The O'Connors may have branded her, but I've got enough photos to show that she's mine. And I've got blankets and food for her that I took from the stables. She'll be all right till then."

Andi bit back the angry words that threatened to burst out of her. Couldn't Sara see the trouble she was in? "Is she still lame?" she asked. They'd never be able to get a lame pony down the farm's steep, stony drive.

"I can't ride her yet, but she can walk OK. She'll be properly better in a couple of days." Sara caught Andi's arm. "Please don't tell anyone where we are. Please!"

"You've got to come back with us, Sara. The O'Connors didn't steal Buttercup, I promise. They bought her from a dealer, who must have been involved with the horse thieves that took her from you. They're really upset that she was stolen." Andi broke off. She couldn't tell Sara everything would be all right, because there was no way of knowing how this would end. But the police were probably heading up here right now; it would look better for Sara if she came back of her own accord.

Sunshine whinnied softly, and Andi went over to

lay her hand against her neck. Her skin felt damp and icy, and she was shivering.

"Poor old girl," Andi said. "She's not happy here, Sara. Look at her, she's cold and wet. You've got to do what's best for her."

"I am! It's best for her to be with me!"

"But not here." Andi swung the torch round, sending the beam over the rubble-strewn floor. "Not in a place like this. Why did you choose to hide here?"

"Because nobody ever comes here. Except you!"

"Look around you," Andi said. "This is no place for a pony. And the rain's getting worse. What if the buildings get washed away altogether?"

Sara gazed round, her face pale and shocked, as though she was seeing her surroundings for the first time. She patted Sunshine's neck. "I'm sorry, girl. I really am."

A halter was hanging on the partition. Andi slipped it over Sunshine's head. "Come on. Let's go." She led Sunshine towards the door. For a moment, Sara stayed where she was, her eyes glistening with unshed tears. Then she followed.

Natalie was waiting outside, sheltering under an

overhang of roof. "Is everything OK?" she asked.

"Yes, Sara's coming back with us."

"Only for Buttercup's sake," Sara added quickly.

It was a brave thing to do, Andi thought, because Sara was going to be in a lot of trouble when they got back. She must love Buttercup very much.

"We've brought Neil's horse, Flash, for you to ride," Natalie told her. "But you'll have to walk down to the end of the road. It's too steep for riding."

Shining the torch ahead, Andi led the way down the track. Water cascaded round her feet, snaking between the rocks. Even the horses found it hard going, moving haltingly over the slippery surface with their ears flat back and their quarters hunched.

When they were halfway down, lightning fizzed across the sky, casting the mountainside in silver light. The horses neighed and shied at the end of their reins.

"Don't let them go!" Andi yelled. Throwing down the torch, she fought to hold on to Chipper, her feet sliding beneath her. The pony plunged wildly, snorting with fear as his hooves sent stones rattling down the slope.

"It's OK, boy. There's nothing to be frightened

of." Andi's heart was pounding, but she managed to speak calmly. To her relief, Chipper stopped pulling and stood still. "Good boy" She patted him, trying to reassure him.

"Are you OK to keep going?" When the others nodded, Andi looked round for the torch. It had rolled into a water-filled gully but, amazingly, it was still working. Andi splashed over to pick it up.

A few metres on, the track levelled out and Natalie drew alongside Andi with Bonnie and Flash. "This is totally different to other lost pets we've found," she said miserably. "Usually everyone's happy, but this just feels horrible, almost as though we've done something wrong."

"I know. I keep wondering what's going to happen to Sara and Sunshine." They reached the grass and Andi turned to call back to Sara. "We can ride from here!" The girl nodded, her face almost white in the shadows, and led Sunshine forward to take Flash from Natalie. She swung herself wordlessly into the saddle and looped Sunshine's reins over the pommel.

Keeping close together, they headed down the slope to the river. Andi wished they could speed up, but it would be dangerous to go too fast in the dark.

"It's a lot deeper than when we crossed before," Natalie said anxiously, peering down at the river.

"The current's faster too," Andi added. The water raced along below Chipper's hooves, frothing against the banks. She stared at the rushing water in dismay. It hardly looked safe to cross, but what other choice did they have? They couldn't spend the night out of doors in this torrential rain. What on earth were they going to do now?

Chapter Twelve

Chipper snatched at the reins and took a step forward.

"What's he doing?" Natalie gasped.

Andi tried to gather up the reins and make him stand still. "Whoa, boy!" she called.

Chipper snorted and scraped at the pebbles under his feet. One or two slipped away and vanished into the churning black water.

"Wait!" said Sara, leaning forward in her saddle. "If he thinks it's safe to cross, you'll have to trust him. Sit still and keep your reins slack, and see what he does."

Andi swallowed hard. She knew Sara was a very experienced rider, but did she know Chipper well enough to trust his judgement about the river? She caught Natalie's eye, and her friend shrugged. There wasn't anyone else around to help them. Taking a deep breath, Andi dropped her hands and let the reins go slack.

With a snort, Chipper put his head down close to the water. Then he leapt into the river and bounded across in three swift strides. Andi gasped and buried her hands in his mane.

"Hold on, Andi!" Natalie shrieked.

But Chipper had already reached the other side and was scrambling out on to the bank.

"We made it!" Andi untangled her fingers from the wiry mane, weak with relief, then turned Chipper so she could shine the torch on to the water. "Come on. It's OK to cross."

Bonnie cantered through the river with Natalie clinging on, but Sunshine balked, pulling the rein taut against Flash's saddle. Sara leant over and ran her hand down the mare's neck. "It's OK, girl," she soothed. "You'll be safe with me." Sunshine looked up at her, her eyes rolling, then lowered her head with a shudder of fear.

Andi watched anxiously. Sunshine was frail and exhausted after her time in the ruined cowshed. She hoped Sara could coax her into the water: they had to cross quickly before the river got any deeper.

"Come on, girl," Sara said. "Do it for me."

Sunshine whinnied, then took a step closer to Flash. Sara straightened up and urged the palomino into the water, twisting in the saddle to check that Sunshine was following. The two horses splashed across, half-trotting, half-cantering, to join Chipper and Bonnie on the lower bank.

"That proves it," Andi said to Natalie. "Sunshine *must* be Buttercup. She was really frightened, but Sara managed to calm her down."

"I know," Natalie agreed. "They've got a real bond." She looked round. "Now we've got to find Neil. Can you remember the way to that boulder, Andi?"

"I think so."

They rode downhill for a little way, then Andi gave a triumphant shout: "There!" The beam of her torch was trembling across the giant rock.

"Natalie, Andi, is that you?" called a voice from the other side. "Did you find Sara and Sunshine?"

"Yes," Natalie replied. "They're here."

Neil struggled to his feet as they rode up to him.

He was still very pale and every movement made him wince.

"I'm really sorry . . ." Sara began through chattering teeth.

"Don't apologize now," Neil interrupted. "What about Sunshine? Is she OK?"

"She bruised her frog on a stone, but she's getting better."

Andi guessed that a frog was part of a horse's hoof. She didn't think Sunshine had adopted any amphibians up at the farm!

Natalie jumped down from Bonnie's back. "I'll give you a bunk up on to Andi's horse." She helped Neil to climb up behind Andi.

"Thanks for coming back for me," he said, slipping one arm round Andi's waist so he wouldn't fall off. "I didn't feel like spending—" He broke off suddenly. "What's that?" Lights had appeared below them, at the edge of the pine woods.

"Neil! Andi! Natalie! Where are you?" a man's voice shouted.

"We're here!" Andi yelled back.

The lights turned in their direction.

"It must be the police," Natalie said.

There were six people in the rescue party. They were dressed in fluorescent orange jackets and they carried ropes and powerful torches. One of them had a first-aid kit slung on his back.

"What on earth do you kids think you're playing at?" demanded one of the police officers. "I couldn't believe it when Mrs O'Connor called to say she thought you'd gone up the mountain. Didn't you notice the weather?"

Before anyone could reply, there was a deafening roar from further up the mountain. "What's that?" Sara screamed.

Every torch turned uphill, and Andi saw a great torrent of foaming, boiling water surging towards them, sweeping rocks and fallen branches ahead of it.

"The river's flooded!" Neil yelled. "Run!"

"We'll be safe in the woods!" the police officer shouted. "There's a gully that will carry the water away before it reaches the trees." He raced down the hill, beckoning for the others to follow him.

Andi clapped her heels against Chipper's sides and galloped down the hill, trying to block out the sound of the floodwater roaring behind her. If it caught them, they'd be swept away and badly injured. And what about Sunshine? She might not be able to outrun the surging water. Neil clung tightly to Andi's waist, his breath coming in painful gasps.

The ponies leapt down into the gully and up the other side, plunging into the trees, where the shadows swallowed them up as if someone had just switched off the light. The riders had overtaken the police officers in their mad gallop, but the men were not far behind now, scrambling up the slope to the trees. The water growled behind them like a bear.

"Come on!" Andi yelled, wheeling Chipper round to watch. To her relief, Sunshine was with them, standing with her head resting on Sara's leg.

The last police officer made it to the top of the gully just as the river poured in behind him, churning and splashing at his heels. There was one dreadful moment when Andi thought the gully might not be deep enough, but then the level of the water fell back as it poured away down the mountain. She let out a long, shaky breath and relaxed her grip on Chipper's reins.

"It's OK, Andi," Neil said quietly. "We made it. Let's go home."

Andi was sitting in the O'Connors' house by the fire, wrapped in a blanket and warming her hands on a mug of hot chocolate, when she heard her mum arrive. She glanced anxiously at Natalie. "We're going to be in terrible trouble."

Mrs Talbot appeared in the living-room doorway, wearing a raincoat and with her hair plastered to her head. "Andi, Natalie – thank goodness you're all right!" She ran over and hugged Andi fiercely. "I couldn't believe it when Mrs O'Connor phoned and told me you'd gone up the mountain in this weather."

"We found them, though, Mum – Sara and Sunshine." Andi looked at Sara over her mum's shoulder, but the girl was staring unhappily into the fire and didn't notice.

"Even so . . ." Mrs Talbot straightened up, and now Andi could see the tension in her face. "You promised me that you wouldn't do anything irresponsible. Suppose the flood had swept you all away?"

"But it didn't, Mrs Talbot. We're fine," Natalie said.

"And I promise we won't do anything like this again," Andi said quietly. She hated the fact that she'd made her mum so worried, and she knew how lucky they were that they hadn't been seriously hurt.

To Andi's relief, the living-room door opened before her mum could say anything else. Mrs O'Connor came in. "Dr Richards is here, Neil. He's waiting in your bedroom to check you over."

"Right." Neil stood up, wincing, and followed her out.

"Good luck," Natalie called after him.

The doorbell rang again. "Can somebody get that, please?" Mrs O'Connor called.

"I will," Andi offered. Glad of something to do to break the tension in the room – she knew her mum was still livid about the danger she and Natalie had put themselves in, even if it was to help Sara and Sunshine – she wrapped her blanket more tightly round her and hurried to the door.

A woman dressed in waterproofs stood there. "I'm Jane Bradley, the vet. Mrs O'Connor called me to look over some ponies that were out in the storm."

Sara came running out of the living room. "I'll show you where they are. One of them, Buttercup, is lame. Can you look at her first, please?"

"Of course."

Sara threw off her blanket, grabbed her sodden coat and raced out into the rain. Andi watched from the door as they disappeared into Sunshine's stable. She wished she knew what was going to happen. Sara would be heartbroken if she had to leave her pony here. And on top of what was happening to Sunshine/Buttercup, Sara was still in big trouble over taking her in the first place. The police had gone back to report to a more senior officer, but Andi wondered if they'd be back later to arrest her. She couldn't bear to think that Sara might be locked up!

The doctor, a smiling grey-haired man, came out of Neil's bedroom with Mrs O'Connor. "Nothing to worry about, Mrs O'Connor, though he'll be pretty sore for a couple of weeks."

Neil's mum looked very relieved. "Thank you for coming, doctor." She held the door for him, then hurried out to speak to the vet.

Andi went back into the living room, suddenly feeling in need of some company. Neil had made it carefully back to his chair and was telling Natalie what the doctor had said – he'd broken his collarbone, but he didn't need to go to the hospital to have it set, luckily.

Andi flopped down on the sofa next to her mum.

"Are you OK, darling?" Mrs Talbot asked.

"I suppose so." It was hard to think that this was yet another successful end to a Pet Finders case. They'd found Sunshine, but had opened a whole can of ugly worms at the same time.

A few minutes later, Mrs O'Connor and Sara came in, shaking raindrops from their hair.

"The horses are fine," Mrs O'Connor announced. "Even Sunshine. I mean, Buttercup . . ." She broke off as they heard a car drive into the yard, and glanced at Sara. "This should be your parents now, I think."

Sara bit her lip and looked down at her hands. Andi felt a pang of sympathy for her. However much trouble she was in with her mum, it was nothing compared with how Sara's parents must be feeling right now. She heard the front door open, then a man spoke. "I'm Mr Morling, Sara's father. Is she here?"

"Yes. Come in." The phone began to ring. "I'll just answer that," Mrs O'Connor said. "Go straight in."

Sara sat up straighter in her chair, staring at the door.

A tall, fair-haired man appeared in the doorway, with an anxious-looking woman behind him. Mrs Walker was there, too, smiling with relief. "Sara!"

Sara stood up, her eyes filling with tears, and ran into her parents' arms. "We've been so worried about you," her mum said, smoothing her hair.

Sara pulled away from them and wiped her eyes on her sleeve. To Andi's surprise, she was looking stubborn rather than upset. "I'm sorry you've been worried, but I'm not sorry I stole Buttercup. She's *my* pony! She should be with me!" Her shoulders slumped. "But I suppose there's no chance of that now."

There was a tense silence. Andi glanced at Neil, wondering if he was going to point out to Sara that his mum had bought Sunshine quite fairly, so she belonged to them now. To her relief, she saw that Neil's eyes were full of sympathy as he looked at Sara.

Mrs O'Connor came in. "That was the police on the phone. Good news, Sara! They've agreed not to press charges, since I told them it wasn't appropriate. You shouldn't have taken Sunshine, but there's no point dwelling on that now."

Sara blinked back tears. "Thanks, Mrs O'Connor," she said in a small voice. "What's going to happen about Buttercup?" she asked, her eyes pleading.

Mrs O'Connor smiled. "Buttercup is *your* pony. I never would have bought her if I'd known she was stolen. I'm sure our insurance policy will cover the money we've lost. Oh, and the police said that the dealer who sold her to us was arrested a few weeks ago for having other stolen horses. He'll be coming up for trial soon."

"Do you really mean it?" Sara asked, beaming so widely that her whole face was one big smile. "I can have Buttercup back?"

"Of course you can."

A great wave of happiness swept over Andi. Everything was going to be all right! The Pet

Finders wouldn't have to regret finding this missing pet after all! She exchanged a triumphant grin with Natalie. "I'll tell you what, Nat, this was definitely our hardest case yet."

"Thank goodness it all turned out all right," Natalie replied. "You can always rely on the Pet Finders to find one thing – drama!"

Andi laughed, feeling suddenly light-headed and full of energy, as though she could run ten miles and still have enough puff for a thousand sit-ups. "You can say that again!"

Mrs Talbot stood up. "It's time we went home," she said, with a sympathetic glance at Sara's family reunion on the other side of the room. Andi and Natalie followed her to the door. "I'm going to be for it when I get home," Andi whispered. "My mum couldn't say much in front of all these people, but I know that look she was giving me. She's going to give me a real talking-to."

"See you next Saturday, Andi," Neil called from the armchair. "I'll try to make sure there are no floods, missing ponies, or runaways to get in the way this time."

For a moment, Andi didn't know what he meant.

Then she remembered she still had the rest of her riding lessons at Riverside Stables. She bet her dad would be amazed to hear what his gift of vouchers had led to! She pretended to frown for a moment. "What, no dangerous mountain rescues and tracking down horse thieves? Hmm, sounds a bit boring." Then she grinned at Neil. "Actually, I can't wait!"

book 7

THE PET FINDERS CLUB

Disappearing Desert Kittens

Do you love animals?
Has your pet ever gone missing?

Well meet Andi, Tristan and Natalie —
The Pet Finders Club. Animals don't stay
lost for long with them hot on the trail!

Andi's supposed to be on holiday but her Pet
Finding instincts take over when she realises
three missing kittens could be in danger!

They may be semi-wild but they're certainly
not big enough to survive on their own!

Can Andi solve the case without the other
Pet Finders there?